The Disgrace
of
Sant' Ambrogio

Memoirs of Father John Conley

SYLVIA HARRISON,
A DANCE & A JOURNY
START WITH ONE STEP.'

Michael Turturici

Michael Turturici

ISBN 979-8-88685-415-2 (paperback)
ISBN 979-8-88685-416-9 (digital)

Christian Faith Publishing
832 Park Avenue
Meadville, PA 16335
www.christianfaithpublishing.com

Printed in the United States of America

Contents

Prologue

I am Father John A. Conley, a forty-year Roman Catholic priest. My Catholic grandparents settled in Boston after immigrating from Northern Ireland. Like so many in the lower classes, they traveled by faith aboard a rusty steamship.

My own search for truth has taken many years and to many countries. I have come to realize of my fellow man, often because of a limited understanding of the spirit. While precariously finding themselves living a mysterious eternal existence, some have found meaning, but only a few have found a true peace with God.

As my days are now fading and my memories still swirl on cool, quiet mornings, I will tell you a story of faith that began at a little church in Florence, Italy. I must retell the beginning of the saga as it was told to me by those who were in the city. It occurred a half a world away and a few short years before I was born.

Florence had suffered many tragedies in its hundreds of years but none in its living memory was worse than that night, the night the bridges were blown. For it was said, "Wherever the German Wehrmacht retreats, they leave a path of destruction."

The Night of the Destruction of the Bridges

August 3, 1944, 7:00 a.m.

As the early morning sun began to climb above the fertile vineyards of Tuscany, the citizens of Florence were being rousted out of their apartments by jackbooted German troops. "Everybody out!" yelled a German sergeant. "Men, women, children, the sick, the elderly, out!"

Doors that did not open were kicked in. And still others were blown to splinters with hand grenades. The panicked citizens who lived all along the river were herded toward the great cathedral Duomo or within the walled Pitti Palace courtyards. Someone shouted, "They're going to destroy our bridges!"

All that day as the sun grew hotter, so did the peoples' anger at the Nazis and anyone who would have collaborated with them. In the sweltering courtyards, bewildered crying children clung to distraught mothers. An old man cursed, *"Il Duce e'un traditore! Mussolini is a traitor!"* He shook his feeble fist in the air. Others came together in circles of prayer. Children's frightened cries echoed between three- and four-story palazzos along Via dei Macci. Their sorrows were carried a few blocks farther from the river by the warm morning breeze to Piazza Ambrogio and the modest church of Sant' Ambrogio.

But the chaos at the river could not be heard through its thick stone walls or the high, narrow stained glass windows of its sanctuary. Its modest stone exterior belied a magnificent single-aisle church with a chapel at the back and four Renaissance side alcoves.

Going back to its Holy Roman roots, Sant' Ambrogio was one of the oldest churches in beautiful Tuscany. Florence had grown up around it decades before the nearby great Duomo di Santa Maria del Fiore was ever conceived. Over the centuries, it had been adorned with artifacts and artworks by some of the masters' medieval sculptures, Renaissance paintings, and fourteenth-century frescoes.

Among its most cherished artworks was a large oil painting on canvas by a contemporary of Michelangelo, Francesco Granacci. At Sant' Ambrogio, there is a marble tomb where Granacci's revered body has lain for six hundred years. Every year, Granacci's oil *Santa Maria* had been taken from the sanctuary's stone wall for the Festa di Santa Maria. The painting was carried at the front of a holy procession. It moved through the city from the church along the narrow Via dei Macci. A carnival atmosphere arose as the people of Florence flocked to the celebration. At Ambrogio's church, the parade had always been a cherished tradition and days of joy.

On that morning of fear and confusion, a humble priest was calmly preparing for the Mass within its sanctuary. Father Danilo Lombardi polished the engraved silver chalice and paten for the offering of Christ's blood and body. The priest had recently been assigned to Sant' Ambrogio. Six months had not been enough time for most of the parishioners to warm up to a new padre. He would have to gain their trust to truly replace the jovial Father Gentile, who had led them in prayer for a generation.

As far as anyone believed, Father Lombardi was Italian but was not Tuscan. Not having been in Florence long enough to have presided over or experienced the Festa di Santa Maria. Not a man of the common people, having been educated in Austria and had curated the arts in Vienna, he was a scholar that curiously spoke fluent German. On the day of confusion, Father Lombardi continued to prepare for the Holy Communion. After that fateful day, many people thought the priest must have known the evening Mass would never take place.

It was still early morning, but Father Lombardi thought better of taking his usual walk to the farmers market. Instead, he received a confession from an elderly woman who wore her black frock and veil. In her ninety-sixth year, she walked slowly gripping a wooden cane, barely lifting herself up the stone steps. She came to confess a minor sin committed long ago. For this, her penance was always light, consisting of a Lord's Prayer recommended by Father Gentile.

After confessions, Father Lombardi was seen at the tomb of Granacci for over an hour, praying in silence. His young assistant Father Bruno attested to this in the dismaying days that followed. Sunlight streaming in through multicolored windows comforted Father Lombardi. He finished his prayer to cease the tragedy unfolding in the river district. The sound of a crying child floated in by what remained of the morning breeze then echoed from the marble floor to the high-glazed windows.

At the open door, a small man appeared, slightly disheveled, hat in hand. He dipped his unsteady hand into a cistern in the portico then hurriedly crossed himself with holy water. From across the sanctuary, he called out, "Father Lombardi!" At the aisle, he knelt and made the sign of the cross. He did this once more as he came closer. He had run almost all the way from the river. Rapidly he breathed and beads of sweat dampened his brow.

"Father Lombardi," he again called out. As usual, the old man was dressed in his thread-worn, loose-fitting suit. He looked like the old farmer that he was. He always sat at the front of the church during Sunday Mass and in that same black suit. "Padre, I have come with terrible news."

Serenely, Father Lombardi greeted the distraught man, "*Buon giorno, Signore* Corsi. Have you come to pray for the weak and frightened?"

"Forgive me, no. I have come to tell you what I have seen with my own saddened eyes this very morning. Five of our partisans held by the gestapo have been shot in front of the old Roman wall. I have come to warn you of the dangerous rumors being repeated at the farmers market.

"I'm not a partisan, just an old man. I see what an old man sees and hear what an old man hears. The people in the street are suspicious people, and many of them are saying...because you have made a friend with a German officer while our partisans have confessed to you, they say you are the one that collaborated with the gestapo.

"I tried to tell them that this is not possible, but they will not believe. They believe only what they have seen for themselves. It is becoming dangerous for you in the city. If you could do something to show them that you are not what they say you are... maybe it is better if you leave Firenze."

Lombardi looked down at the floor, placed a reassuring hand on Corsi's slumping, shoulder, then quietly answered, "A man of faith would say, faith reveals what a man does not see."

The old man could only respond with uncertainty in his eyes. Lombardi seemed to understand this. He said, "Kneel with me, *Signore*. Let us pray for peace."

The prayer comforted *Signore* Corsi, though sadly, he knew the people would not forgive those sins so easily. Father Lombardi finished the prayer, saying, "Thank you for your prayers, *Signore*.

Now there are things I must prepare for." He escorted the old farmer back to the portico. "God go with you."

Before Corsi walked beyond the open door, he again crossed himself, stared directly at the priest, lamenting, "I have not the faith that I should have. Forgive me, Father."

A few hours later, Father Lombardi called Father Bruno into his study. There was a letter written by him on the desk. "Did you hear the news brought by *Signore* Corsi?"

"I could not help overhearing it. This very morning at the market, the people seemed strange toward me. Some looked away from my eyes."

"I see...though I'm sad to hear it," said Father Lombardi. "Of course, I would not want you to suffer under my dark shadow."

"It's a shadow I would gladly fall under, Monsignor. You are a man of God, or he surely would not have chosen you to lead this church. But I am also troubled by the rumors. What am I to believe?"

Father Lombardi stood behind his desk now more resolute in what he had to do. "I have written a letter to the bishop. The truth is in it. I want you to deliver it to him at the Vatican, for the bishop only. For this, you must leave imminently."

Father Bruno thought for a moment. "But how can I go to Rome? The trains have been wrecked. I would have to cross through German lines."

"You can still travel west to Pisa and there cross the Arno to the holy city."

"Do you think it's wise for you to stay here alone? I mean, with all that's going on in the city, the bridges being blown, angry partisans hiding behind every corner, waiting for the Germans' retreat to the north?"

Father Lombardi, irritated and flustered by Bruno's hesitation, raised his voice, "Go! Deliver this message. Go quickly. Leave this city before it's too late."

Father Bruno was visibly shocked by his priest's abrupt response. "While I know you are under a great stress, this is not like you."

What Father Lombardi said next puzzled his assistant even more. "It would be wise for you to wait for the Germans to evacuate Florence before you return. If I am not here, no harm can befall you. The letter will explain why I have sent you."

Father Bruno could not know what was in the letter or the urgency to hurry it to Rome. He said, "Then I will do as you demand. I will leave within the hour. Upon my return, we can only hope this dark cloud will have gone with the Germans."

"May God go with you, Father Bruno."

After Bruno had left, the remaining priest slowly closed the bronze doors of the empty church and locked it with a heavy iron bolt.

The sweltering day wore on. Wehrmacht engineers efficiently wired the bridges with high explosives. By late afternoon, all residents from the river district had been moved, detained, and quarantined. The hot August sun began to melt beyond the hills. German troops casually patrolled deserted streets or lingered in the empty gathering places. At the Piazza Ambrosio, plain-clothed men of the gestapo sat at a shaded cafe table, keeping in clear view of the church…watching…waiting.

*****

Well after sunset, most German troops had already moved north to the Gothic Line. At last, the partisans had their chance for revenge, for just as the gestapo had been surveilling the church, so had they. Abruptly, the running clap of heavy boots on cobble-stone streets was heard closing in around the church. Italian partisans came for battle. They knew this house of God had already been occupied by their well-armed enemy. Flanking the front steps were six or seven Germans standing guard. There were two more standing around a canvas-covered truck parked adjacent to the rear door.

Every tall candle had been lit in the peaceful sanctuary. Stained glass glowed in the night. Because of this, Father Lombardi was seen by the Italian partisans through the open door. And dishonoring the sanctuary was Gestapo Colonel Ziegler, who, at dawn, had ordered the execution of their comrades at the Roman wall.

The first shot cracked as an Italian bullet found a German soldier standing on the terrace. His lifeless body rolled down the stone steps to the ground. A startled corporal ordered, "Take cover! Return fire!" He called into the sanctuary, "Colonel, we are under attack."

Several more shots flew in both directions. An angry partisan yelled, "We want the traitor Lombardi!"

Another fuming voice called out, "Lombardi the collaborator."

The Germans quickly scrambled behind their trucks. They fired at partisan guns that flashed in the shadows. One more battle, baptized in blood, echoed among the ancient stone walls. There was only one thing that could have stopped the fighting, and that would mean the end of Father Lombardi.

At precisely 9:50 p.m., the first explosion felt like an earthquake. An apocalyptic fireball lit up the night sky, reflecting red flame on astonished upturned faces. Secured windows shattered into empty apartments. Art galleries and civic buildings shook to their stone foundations. Screams and cries from six thousand confined citizens rose above the city. The fireball could be seen in the city of San Paulo eighteen kilometers away. The Ponte Santa

Trinita, the beautiful bridge of Florence that had spanned the Arno River for over six hundred years, had been completely destroyed.

The gunfight paused for a moment, but not one person inside Sant' Ambrogio showed themselves. A dozen more German troops arrived. The partisans had no choice but to move back into the shadows. Germans quickly secured the plaza, so no one could see what was being loaded into the canvas-covered carrier that had backed up to the door.

It wasn't long before the vehicle was loaded. To the astonishment of those who observed it, Father Lombardi and Captain Mueller climbed into Ziegler's staff car. It sped away, disappearing into the dark night. The covered truck followed close behind.

Throughout the long night, four more explosions rumbled buildings and cobblestone streets, one explosion every hour and one more bridge erased. Ponte Carraia, Grazie, Vespucci, San Niccolò—demolished. The last bridge was gone by 3:00 a.m. Only the beautiful Ponte Vecchio was spared but made impassable by destroying the buildings on both sides of the river to block American tanks from advancing north.

At dawn, the people, no longer detained, cautiously moved away from the Pitti Palace. The German army had drifted away just as black smoke had drifted away from the city. They went to the river to see their cherished bridges, but all that remained of the five beautiful bridges were broken dams of smoldering rubble.

Assignment at
the Vatican

Vatican City, September 22, 1978

Deep within the vast halls of the Vatican, two clerical priests contemplated a young priest from Boston and the church of Sant' Ambrogio. Perhaps a young Irish American priest could breathe new life into the forgotten church. They would have to explain the disgrace of Sant' Ambrogio to the young Father John Conley, with a hope he would embrace it as his first parish.

*****

Here, I will continue the saga, as only I can tell it. After a long flight from Boston to Rome, I took the underground to the Vatican and made my way to a chamber door. "Come in, Father Conley, come in. How was your flight?"

With a joyful smile, I answered, "It was long and prayerful, Monsignor."

"The Vatican will always be your home," said Monsignor DeLuca. Sifting through a folder laid out on an ancient wooden desk, he said, "I see here you have a bachelor's degree from UCLA, played baseball—"

"It was right field."

"You attended seminary in Boston, and you wish to study the arts here at the Vatican?"

I respectfully replied, "Yes, Monsignor."

Then Father Moretti spoke. "Let's get down to our purpose. You are anticipating your first assignment at the Vatican, which is always in need of young enthusiastic priests. Let's talk about a modest church in Florence in need of revitalization."

Monsignor DeLuca took over. "For thirty-four years, Father Bruno has been the resident pastor of a once-revered church in Florence. We are looking for someone like yourself to assist Father Bruno until he retires, his position to advance to a younger pastor. But before we assign you, we felt you should be informed as to the circumstances concerning that sanctuary, past and present."

Father Moretti glumly added, "You see, Sant' Ambrogio is in disgrace, a disgrace that over many years has made Father Bruno lose his enthusiasm for the parish."

They must have noticed my concern. Monsignor DeLuca went on, "Sant' Ambrogio was a glorious church, built by Saint Ambrose in the fourth century outside the city. Over the following centuries, Florence grew around it. It became the center of the community, spiritual life, and holy festivals. Yes, greater cathedrals were later built, but Sant' Ambrogio remained most favored by many."

I could only sincerely inquire, "May I ask, what is this disgrace?"

Monsignor DeLuca slowly stepped to the east window that overlooked the plaza straight across to the towering monument of Saint Peter. "Let me tell you what we know. It is said by many that during the last days of the German occupation of Florence, Father Lombardi had been collaborating with the gestapo. As a result, several Italian resistance fighters, exposed by the traitor Lombardi, were caught and executed."

Father Moretti continued the disheartening saga, "On the night the Germans destroyed the bridges in Florence, Father Lombardi fled the city with the Germans. He has not been seen again. What is worse, they stole Granacci's oil *Saint Mary*. Since that day, the Festa di Santa Maria has not graced the streets of Florence."

Again, respectfully, I asked, "This disgrace, can it be forgiven?"

Father Moretti sadly replied, "Go to Sant' Ambrogio. Talk to Father Bruno. Many years have passed. Your appointment has been arranged with the bishop of Florence. You will see him on Tuesday. It is our hope He will work a miracle through your hands, and faith will be renewed. We have every confidence that God will guide you."

*****

I found myself walking through the gilded halls of the Vatican Art Museum on my way to the venerable city of Florence. It was my first visit to Italy. So far, I had only seen the airport and taken the public rail to the Vatican, a place I'd dreamed about seeing since joining seminary.

So far, my journey to Italy had been a whirlwind. I was actually at the Vatican. Pope John Paul II was there! I felt like a schoolboy on the adventure of his life. I might even see the Holy Father in a hallway or praying in the Sistine Chapel. In that chapel, I asked God for modesty under Michelangelo's *The Creation of Adam*. I ambled through the inspiring pope's church, Saint Peter's Basilica.

Tuscan Vineyards
to Florence

Father Moretti had given me a Vatican driver's license and use of a blue 1966 Fiat 500, the kind with the lawn mower engine in the rear. After the cryptic meeting at the Vatican, the drive through the winding roads of Tuscany was both refreshing and beautiful, a deep blue sky was spotted with puffy white clouds. Farmers in the vineyards, with their labor, picked and hauled purple grapes in the sun.

Intending to browse a farmer's market in the hilltop village of San Donato, I lingered there for a precious hour. My gaze scanned the faraway olive orchards and colorful vineyards that carpeted the hillsides. My spirit was free, floating above the ageless valley. I could not help reflecting on the millennia of peace or war in what remains of ancient Rome and the Tuscans before that. But what about the farmers and shopkeepers who had labored on the hillsides, in the villages of unknown memories lost? I traveled on.

*****

After a long day's drive, with the crimson sunset low over the hills, the Fiat putted into the outskirts of Florence. I made my way down the Via dei Macci to the old Roman plaza of Sant' Ambrogio. At twilight, the plazas came alive in the city. By eight o'clock, crowds of citizens mingled in the streets, cafés were busy as were the pastry and gelato shops. I tightly parked the Fiat among the countless motor scooters lining a narrow street. It was just around the corner from the center of Plaza Sant' Ambrogio.

People sat on the church's steps, reading or enjoying their gelato. With them absorbed into a temperate mood of the plaza, my entering the church caused little attention. Facing the church, I wondered what it might have been like in 1944.

In a pointed arch above the bronze doors, there was a fresco of Mary holding the infant Jesus. Carved into the granite header above the door was the word "Rispetto," meaning reverence. And reverently, I crept through the doorway. Peering inside, tall multi-colored windows and tenth-century pillars lined a darkened portico. In the vestibule, I dipped my fingers into a cistern of holy water then made the sign of the cross.

At the far end of the colonnade, a lone laboring priest silently lit altar candles in front of a surprisingly beautiful marble taber-nacle. I progressed around the center of the portico between the outer wall and walnut pews, only pausing for a moment at the ornate tomb of the Renaissance painter Francesco Granacci. My call echoed across the empty space. "Excuse me. Father Bruno?"

A step into the dim light revealed a tired face. "I am Father Bruno."

Optimistically, I moved toward him holding out my hand. "I'm Father Conley. I've been—"

He cut me short. "I know who you are. You've come to replace me, and you couldn't have come sooner"

Hoping for a positive beginning, I respectfully asked, "How may I assist you, Father Bruno?"

He was unimpressed. "Assist me…you think that is why they sent you?" Annoyed, he abruptly demanded, "Why did you want to be a priest, Father Conley?"

From memory, I confidently responded, "To do good works and help others have faith."

"Oh, I understand. I was once a young enthusiastic priest full of faith. My father wanted me to be a doctor. If I had, I could have saved lives. As it is, I couldn't even save myself, let alone this dying church." Looking a bit remorseful at the way he'd treated me, he said, "Well, hmm, come with me to the rectory, young pastor. Sister Charlene is there. She may have something for us to eat."

*****

By late October, I had settled into life in Florence. There were few weddings and baptisms at Sant'Ambrogio, so I had some time to peruse the art museums. One afternoon, while wandering the halls of the Uffizi Gallery, from its Greek sculptures to lifeless flat paintings of the Dark Ages, I entered a room where paintings were suddenly full of life. the Renaissance was in full display in the astounding human expression in Michelangelo's *Holy Family with St. John the Baptist*. Francesco Granacci was a contemporary of the great painter and knew him well. There were similarities in my church. With this inspiration, I could bring a rebirth, a resurrection to my sermons as the Renaissance had brought new life to Florence so long ago.

I walked to another gallery to see *David*, the artist's greatest achievement. Carved out of a single eighteen-foot-high block of marble. The David, who killed Goliath with a sling, Michelangelo's inspiring, lifelike sculpture goes to the heart of the Renaissance. It is told that David represents the break from the bondage of superstition to the God-given freedoms of the new man. I spent hours at the galleries and was myself renewed in spirit.

*****

There are no big box stores in the old city of Florence. On the ground level of three- or four-story palazzos, there are small shops that line the way. A bread baker here, a pasta maker there, a tiny café on the corner. Each morning, except Sundays, I walked to the farmers market. Fresh tomatoes, beans, garlic, and all other types of goods are haggled for. At dawn, the vendors were busy setting out their wares on makeshift tables placed under colorful plastic awnings. What was a daily routine for them was a joyous morning for a young New England priest.

I was greeted by the old men bantering on the benches and sat among them. They talked about old woman and sometimes the young ones that walked by. I invited them to Sundays sermon. A short-haired brown cat jumped up onto my lap and nudged for a scratch behind the ear. He, too, was making new friends.

My apartment was on the top floor of a four-story palazzo adjacent to the church. Its pale-green kitchen shutters overlooked the city past the Duomo at Santa Maria del Fiore all the way to the river. There were great opera singers, posing as venders or cab drivers. A street merchant on a corner sang *Rigoletto* as he wrapped bunches of red crocuses in a newspaper.

In the warmth of the afternoon, an old man walked past his window in his birthday suit, and no one seemed to notice. Perhaps, he'd found his peace with God in this nakedness. A woman across the way tended an incredibly beautiful balcony flower garden. On a terrace, after 9:00 p.m., a loud, wonderful large family gathered for dinner. The friendly Italian cat from the market had made a habit of jumping through my kitchen window. With the help of a small cup of milk and a few morsels of leftover cod, I seemed to have made a friend of this sovereign cat.

At sunset, the breeze turned cool as the sun's last red cinder died out below a distant mountain peak. As the city darkens, the plaza came alive again. People fill the plaza, ready for supper or dessert, or just to watch other people having supper or dessert. It went on late on warm nights. Sometimes, after midnight, under the glow of a romancing moon, young friends and lovers sharing that last bottle of red wine strolled away.

*****

On Friday mornings, three Catholic nuns made their way eight blocks from Cathedral Santa Maria del Fiore to the relatively tiny church of Sant' Ambrogio. As they briskly moved ahead, they reminded me of three black-and-white geese in a row, Sister Charlene always in front of the string. It was a welcome reprieve from the daily monotony of my tasks. Sometimes they brought school children, excited to be out of school.

While enjoying my usual breakfast of cappuccino and pastry, the nuns marched up the stone steps. Showing them deference, I'd say, "Good morning, sisters."

They'd respond, "Buon giorno, Father Conley."

The other sisters would go straight into the sanctuary. They were always about their duties; they came to support the church and refresh the rectory, making sure Father Bruno had what he required to sustain Sant'Ambrogio for one more week. The nuns worked together efficiently and quietly, for they had much more to do when they returned to the great cathedral, Santa Maria del Fiore.

Sister Charlene was a strong woman from the forested foothills of the Italian Alps. She had given her life to Christ at a young age. Seemingly stern, once past her iron will, Sister Charlene had a kind, giving soul. She was not one to hold back the truth when she thought it was needed. If anything, I could trust she'd do that!

*****

The days of summer swiftly drifted by. The first week of November brought dark clouds and cold rain. On a Friday, a welcome sun warmed the red tile roofs crowning the city. Over the past three months, I had done my best to bring new patrons to Sant' Ambrogio, but few were interested in discussing the disgraced church. With a resolute heart, I had tried, but I couldn't shake the sinking feeling that my mission would ultimately fail.

There was only one other person that I could count on to give me the truth. I waited for Sister Charlene to finish her usual prayer at the altar. "God be with you, sister."

"And with you," she returned.

"Sister Charlene, do you mind if I ask how long you have been coming to Sant' Ambrogio?"

"It has been six dedicated years, Father Conley, less a month."

"And do you know my mission?"

"I think the Vatican's view of your mission may have changed."

"Changed? In what way? I've heard nothing. As far as I know, it is the same as it was the day I was assigned. I ask you because I thought, with your advice, we could bring Sant' Ambrogio back to life."

She explained, "I am bewildered, Father Conley. We were under the impression that our duties would end once the church had become an auxiliary to the Santa Maria del Fiore. There will be no more services at this sanctuary, only special events and conferences."

She commented on her common belief resolutely. "It's probably better that way. When Father Bruno retires, this church will no longer be holding services."

I clutched the silver crucifix at the end of my rosary. "But these must be only rumors. If the Vatican had made that decision, surely I would have been told!"

She thoughtfully suggested, "They could be just rumors. That is not known for sure. But everyone knows this church is under a dark cloud and will always be."

I was dumbfounded. I'd come from Boston, where people no longer believed in curses and superstitions. "You certainly don't believe that?"

"It doesn't matter what I think. The people of Florence believe it, and they haven't changed in more than thirty-four years. No, Father Conley, I tell you, this church will be closed. It might as well be engraved on its old stone walls."

*****

I glanced at my wristwatch; it was one in the afternoon. Most likely, Father Bruno would be lingering in the rectory. Being young and in a hurry, in a few seconds, I bound up three flights of brick stairs and opened the door to the residence. The retiring priest contently sat at the kitchen table. A fresh breeze mildly wafted into the apartment through the open window. On the table, he had prepared a cup of tomato-basil soup and a loaf of day-old bread; in his hand, a glass of old Chianti.

Without looking away from his gaze through the window, with a warm expression, he said, "Sit with me. Have a glass of vino?"

I sat across the table. "*Graze*, Father Bruno."

He begun to pour some red wine into an empty coffee cup. "You know, I have been drinking a little more these days."

As he returned to his gaze above the tile rooftops, he reached out his hand, pointing to the far sanguine green mountains to the north. "See there, just below the tall peak, there in the green meadow—the Abbey Monticello." He took an assuring drink from his half-full glass. "I'll soon be casting for trout in those cold-water steams. Look there. You can see the way the sun has broken through the clouds?"

It was good to see him smile. "I hope it gives you comfort, Father Bruno, that your retirement will bring you a long-awaited solace."

As we sat together in that little kitchen, he was so far away. He talked of Monticello as if he'd been walking through a beautiful long-lost dream. After a while, he drifted back to his bread and wine. I also lifted my cup. We sat in silence for what seemed like a long while. "Father Bruno, I also have a dream."

He looked into me with his deep gray eyes. "Yes, I know. I know, my son, just as I had mine as a young priest."

I lifted my cup without taking a drink. Swiftly setting it down, I said, "I'm sorry, Father Bruno. I realize now that I've been a fool. Who did I think I was to be the one to come along and change everything in this place in a few months? Sister Charlene thinks the Mass will end, and Sant' Ambrogio will remain open only for sightseers."

Placing his glass on the table, he looked for the far meadow and prophesized, "For a time, perhaps years, sightseers will make their way to this sanctuary. But this is an old church! Someday, when the memory of my generation or the next has finally gone, well, who knows?"

Pausing for a moment, I asked the burning question, the one I'd been reluctant to ask from the first moment I'd seen him. "There were many stories told about the priest that took the painting. Father Bruno, may I ask you…what happened that August night?"

With an agreeable look on his weathered face, he slowly stood up from the table, carrying the empty bowl and bread plate to the sink. "What does it matter anymore? After all these years, I will tell you what I can remember. I will tell you because after I leave this church, I will want to forget."

He turned on the spigot and waited for the water to run hot. "As you know, I was Father Lombardi's young assistant." He smiled as he remembered. "At the time, I was even younger than you. Oh, Sant'Ambrogio was a wonderful place before the war. It was a place of hope, and because of that, thousands of joyous people attended the holy festivals."

The smile faded from his face. "Then the Germans came! At first, they left us alone, only coming to the sanctuary as tourists taking snap shots. But why not, Mussolini was allied with Hitler."

As he cleaned the dishes in soapy hot water, he remembered more. "Because they had a common interest in the arts, it seemed Father Lombardi made a friend of a German officer. Soon after Italy surrendered to the Americans, things got worse. Italian partisans who resisted were revealed to the gestapo. It was suspected Father Lombardi had betrayed them to his German friend."

I wondered aloud, "Did anyone know this for a fact?"

He then said something that astonished me: "I don't know. In suspicious times, suspicions often are seen as reality."

"Is it true? Did Father Lombardi and the German disappear with the painting?"

"As I have testified many times, I can't say. Lombardi had sent me to the Vatican to deliver a letter. As it happened, I was not in Florence."

"Father Bruno, do you remember the name? Who was his German friend?"

The old priest rubbed his stubbled chin to focus his memory. "Mueller. I'm sure of it." He shut off the water as he sputtered. "Capt. Frederick Mueller! It was all so many years ago, and old memories most fortunately have drifted away."

The old priest retired to his chamber while I was left gazing at a lonesome gray faraway cloud drifting. I had to get out, so I bounced down the stone stairway, feeling dismayed. My body burst through the bottom doors into the sunlight and quickly crossed the crowded lane, entering the church through the same obscure side door the gestapo had taken decades before.

*****

My New England upbringing taught me to never give up unless it was practical! I was torn between my dedication to the church and plain common sense. I felt a need for guidance and was compelled toward the altar. Overwhelmed with heavy emotions and clutching my crucifix for comfort, I began a silent prayer.

> In the name of the Father and of the Son and of the Holy Spirit... Father, I have taken my vows and worn the robes joyfully. I thought my appointment to Sant' Ambrogio was a blessing. I feel now it is a trial. But it is Your will that gives purpose to all life. I've done everything to fulfill my mission here, but things have not gone well. If You could show a way, open a door. I will do all possible to change the hearts of those without faith in this church.

As I prayed, the afternoon sun moved into position, so from a high window, a beam of white light caressed the image of our Savior above the altar. Not expecting an answer, I lowered my head as my doubts rushed in. There came a sound clear and pure as the light that shined on the image of God. Was it only my desire to hear it whisper? "If you would have faith, it will be done."

"But how, Lord? What can be done?"

Only silence, but in that silence, a calm descended within my spirit. That sweet voice had come from the high beams above the sanctuary and the depths of my soul. I had heard the sound before in a pine forest in Maine. When I was a boy of ten, I was lost for three days and nights in the deep woods. God was with me then in every tree and meadow. I heard Him long before I decided to become a priest. Years later, it became clear why there was no reply. Then it was certain He had given me the responsibility to save the church of Sant' Ambrogio.

I meditated on this for a while. Suddenly, there was the presence of someone somewhere in the church. I scanned the dark corners of the sanctuary, and silhouetted by candlelight, a small figure was kneeling at the devotional. I recognized her by our familiarity. It was Signora Rosalie Campinella, the oldest living disciple of Sant' Ambrogio.

I quietly went to her as she lit another red prayer candle for an anguished soul. "God be with you, signora."

Her spirit had been lifted up and dragged down many times. The beauty of her youth had long passed. In her ninety-sixth year, her indomitable faith was alive and well. She looked into my eyes. Her smile brought the hope of everlasting life. As she spoke, I felt her warmth. "Father Conley, will you take my confession?"

Separated by the screen of the confessional, we prayed. Somehow, I knew she wanted to talk, or was it what I wanted? I had to know from her perspective, for it was her long-earned wisdom I desperately required. "Signora Campinella, how long have you been a patron of Sant' Ambrogio?"

Her sincere voice came clearly through the curtain. "Father Conley, all my life! I was baptized and married here. For ten generations, all my families were baptized in this sanctuary. This is my family's church and mine. As long as I live, I will never abandon Sant' Ambrogio."

"What was it like in the old days? Was Sant' Ambrogio as glorious as they say?"

Without hesitation, memories of her contented childhood came back. "We looked forward to the festival every year. All the people anticipated the procession of the *Santa Maria*. So many people eating, praying, celebrating the blessings—its memory clings to me in my morning dreams. My older brother Giovanni was killed by the gestapo. It all ended when the disgrace of Father Lombardi gripped the hearts of the people."

Now I was behind the curtain confessing to her. "Signora Campinella, before, when at the altar praying for guidance, God's voice came softly to me. Has He ever spoken to you? Have you heard His voice?"

"Yes! Many times. He has guided me throughout my life. He is always speaking to the ones who hear Him."

"You say He has spoken to you. Tell me...what can be done to bring back this church? At the altar, just a while ago, He clearly said it was my mission."

"Father Conley, God's plan is hidden behind a black veil, a veil of life, the veil of death. It is hidden because He wants us to have faith. Your question has been contemplated long before the Vatican sent you to Florence. If you believe you have come to revive the church, you must follow His will, His *volere*. There is only one way to let the people believe in this church again."

"How can it be?"

"To remove the veil, retrieve the painting of *Santa Maria!*" The hope in her voice burned through the curtain. "I have longed to see it leading the procession again before He takes me. You have a sure heart. Do this for faith."

Knowing the way was clear, the key to reviving the church now seemed simple. Just find Granacci's painting of Saint Mary. Bring it back, and light would again shine on Sant' Ambrogio.

More than three decades had passed. Thousands of artifacts captured by the Nazis were still missing. Some were undoubtedly hidden in private collections. Tragically, countless fine works of art have been lost or destroyed by widespread bombing and overall destruction. Yes, many had been recovered and returned to their rightful owners, but those recoveries had, of late, been few and far between. I suddenly was beginning to feel like that child—again lost alone in a wilderness.

*****

There was only one place to start: where it had begun—at the Vatican. By phone, Father Bruno set up a meeting with Monsignor DeLuca and Father Moretti. I had been given permission to travel there the next available day. The Fiat had been taken back to the Vatican, so I boarded the train that traveled a few hours south through the wine country from Florence to Rome. I caught the underground rail across Rome, then over the river Tiber to the holy city.

With open arms and a wide smile, Father Moretti greeted me at the chamber door. "*Buon pomeriggio*, Pastor Conley."

His enthusiastic hug took me by surprise. "And good afternoon to you, Father Moretti."

Monsignor DeLuca was also welcoming as he reached across the big oak desk to warmly shake my hand. "Please, sit here, where we can talk."

A nun quietly placed a silver tray holding a steaming crystal carafe and a set of earthen cups on a small table within the

Monsignor's reach. "In your impression, how is Father Bruno, young priest?"

"He talks now of fishing the clear streams about Abbey Monticello. He's changed! I think he's mellowed."

Father Moretti recited, "In Acts, it says, 'May I finish my course with joy, testifying the gospel of the grace of God.'"

DeLuca asked, "We have chamomile tea. Will you have a cup?"

"*Si, grazie.*"

As Monsignor DeLuca filled a cup of the golden liquid, he said, "Speaking of Father Bruno, our telephone conversation with him was short. He only told us that you had something to ask about the church. He wished us well, almost farewell, then abruptly said goodbye."

"When first meeting you here at the Vatican, we were in one accord, that my internship at Sant' Ambrogio could lead to revival. Now I think moods have changed. I have been told by the sisters that Sant' Ambrogio, as a church, will be abandoned. Is it true? Will it be open only for tourists? I came to hear it from you!"

Father Moretti glanced at Monsignor DeLuca, sadly confirming, "It is true."

It felt like the bottom had fallen from my spirit. "Is there anything that can be done?"

"I'm afraid no, young pastor. The power is out of our hands. But I'm sure you believe it when I say when one door is closed, the Holy Father will open another."

There was a pause in the conversation while we sipped the soothing tea. "Monsignor DeLuca, Moretti, there may be a door that can be opened. Have you heard of a Frederick Mueller?"

Curiously, Monsignor DeLuca inquired, "No, the name is not familiar. Do you know of this person, Father Moretti?"

Silence. It was my time to speak. "We all know Father Lombardi had made a German friend. That man was there at the church on the night of the destruction of the bridges. He was with the gestapo and Father Lombardi when they fled north with the irreplaceable painting. That man was Capt. Frederick Mueller."

DeLuca asked, "This man, can he be your open door?"

"Indulge my speculation for a moment. If Mueller survived the war and is still alive, he would be in his seventies. If he can be found, it is conceivable that he could give us at least some information regarding the painting."

Monsignor DeLuca, seeing the opening, offered, "The Vatican archives hold countless wonders. As it happens, military personnel records from many countries are kept in its vaults. Father Moretti can take you down beneath the subfloors below the basilica. In the archives, you may find the records you are looking for regarding this Captain Mueller. We will pray for a *viaggio friuloso*, a fruitful journey."

Father Moretti opened the door into the hall, saying, "Follow me, Father Conley. I will open your eyes to the history of the world."

We walked together through the adorned halls to a restricted elevator, where tourists' access was not allowed. As the elevator continued lower and lower, Moretti said, "The archives are on this third level, but first, I want to take you down to the lowest places under Saint Peter's, to the ancient catacombs."

"The catacombs?" My palms were starting to sweat, and I was getting that uneasy feeling. My claustrophobia started to kick in at the thought of going still lower.

Finally, we hit bottom, and the doors opened to a narrow low cavern. We crept down past many early Christian graves. In the damp, silent crypt, the only sound was a trickle of water coming from somewhere in the depths. My fear of tight places was closing in, but making the sign of the cross, I followed Father Moretti down an ever-narrowing shaft.

Ultimately, we came to an excavation site. "Look, here," he whispered, "carved into the stone, a cross that is upside down." In a small place below the inverted cross were half-uncovered bones. "Here in Latin, the name Peter the Apostle."

My fears of tight places quickly evaporated at the sight of the tomb. He told me more. "It is believed that this is the very spot Saint Peter was crucified over two thousand years ago. The pope's church was built on top of it. Our Savior Jesus Christ truly made Peter the rock, the foundation of His church."

After praying in the catacombs, we decided to walk up the old stone stairways to the archives. An attending pastor located the section where German army records were stored. Father Moretti wished me luck and headed toward the elevator.

The following days were consumed with poring over boxes of German military records, which served to only confirm that Mueller was a very common name. I resolutely settled into my work. In 1944, there were over two hundred Frederick Mueller's in the Wehrmacht. Hours dragged by. Doggedly searching paper records and microfilm, I found only one Capt. Frederick Mueller who served in Italy. To my surprise, he was not gestapo. He was with the foreign office. Maybe a spy? His last known residence was in Heidelberg.

At the first opportunity, Monsignor DeLuca lent me the same old Fiat 500, the one without a working speedometer or horn. I began the treacherous journey over the Alps, headed to Heidelberg, Germany, in winter.

*****

An ominous, dark frigid storm blanketed the way over the Italian Alps that night. A radio announcer warned that an avalanche had blocked the autostrada to Switzerland and advised travelers to take shelter till morning. The radio crackled for the last time before moving out of range. I wondered if the little Fiat could get over the old pilgrim road. My mission and sure heart compelled me, perhaps foolishly, to take the way up to the monastery of Saint Benedict.

The road to the summit was getting colder. Soft snow swirled, causing ice to freeze on the windshield. Looming high peaks were now masked in darkness. The car puttered through a howling winter wind with dim headlights to lamp the icy road only a few feet ahead.

As the little car climbed to an elevation of eight thousand feet, I remembered a single sign an hour past, reading, "PETROL STAZIONE." There had been no gas for at least forty miles. Then by the grace of God, as the wind battered the steamed-up windshield, a light appeared in the mist, and my spirit gladdened. Glancing nervously at the gas gauge with less than a quarter tank remaining, I planned to top off the tank to make it all the way up to the monastery. To my dismay, the car rolled off the road into a closed deserted station. No gas!

I had to get my bearings, so I apprehensively pulled the flashlight and map out of the glove compartment. According to the map, Saint Benedict was at nine thousand feet in elevation or twenty-seven thousand meters. I scribbled the math on the edge of the map: three thousand meters higher and forty miles to go! At that point there was no turning back.

Slipping the small wheels into gear, my little heated sanctuary continued farther up the frozen highway. Thoughts swirled in my mind like the snow swirled on the road. *What about Captain Mueller? Would he have any clue what happened to the painting?*

He'd be an old man by now, if he's still around. How long could a man live carrying that sort of burdensome past? Would I find him in Heidelberg, or would that be the end of my journey?

Old memories drifted back to pleasant days in Maine sitting around a campfire. At dusk, when the sky turned gray brushed by streaks of crimson clouds, birds signaled the coming of night. When the last glow of sunset fades beneath peaks, we light our campfire and call it magic hour. Dad taught me to always bring a thermos filled with hot coffee or chocolate on our ice fishing trips. I had come prepared for the snow on the Alps with a heavy hooded jacket, thermal underwear, and a thermos filled with café Americana. Though the old Fiat was not the best way to get through a snowstorm, at least it had a nice, warm heater.

So as my recollections drifted back to Maine, the car drifted to the edge of the roadway, slowly sliding sideways toward the abyss of a mountain cliff far above an icy river. A thin layer of ice coated the highway, so slamming on the brakes might put the car into a slide over the edge. The only thing to do was to stick the car into neutral and keep my foot off the brake. At the cliff's edge, the passenger-side tires bounced off a low asphalt berm, surely preventing disaster, and the car rolled neatly to a slow stop.

I hung my head on the steering wheel and scolded myself. *Should have waited until the storm passed. Don't want to have to explain to Monsignor DeLuca that somewhere in the Alps, the car was stuck in a snowbank or worse. Just keep it on the road!*

Shifting it back into gear, the engine idled slowly through drifting snow and fog. It moved away from the ledge and continued the climb toward the summit. It nudged around curve after curve, switchback after switchback. I stopped now and then to wipe off the fog on the windshield with an extra undershirt. I could only guess if there was enough petrol left to make the summit. There were no lights or signs ahead, nothing to give a clue how much farther to the monastery. Icy wind swayed ghostly white pines all around. The gas gauge was already bouncing off empty. The little engine was running on fumes.

The Abbey of Saint Benedict

So dark the road, so thick the snow, I drove right past the gate to the monastery of Saint Benedict. I slid to a stop, backed up, and turned onto the drive, feeling very lucky. Warm colorful light streaming from the cathedral reminded me of a Christmas tree. I parked the car, pulled my coat tightly around my chest, and battled the howling wind into the abbey, causing a rush of cold air to burst into the room.

A joyful monk gave the standard greeting. "Welcome, pilgrim, to the abbey of Saint Benedict. May it be your refuge on this treacherous night."

"*Tante grazie*—glad to be here!"

As he helped pull off my heavy coat and scarf, he could plainly see that this was one cold, wet, and exhausted pilgrim. Peering out the window, he politely asked, "By the grace of God, you came in that?"

Responding with an ironic grin, I said, "It seems the Vatican didn't have a snowmobile."

He looked a little puzzled at my American wit, but he beamed as he quickly got the joke. We both laughed. "Well, come in. You will brave no more snow while at the abbey. This has been a place of refuge for—"

As he spoke, my eyes were fixed across the lobby on a huge red-hot blazing hearth. He rightly noticed that I was fading. "First things first. Come, sit by the fire."

Warmed by the hearth, gulping down two cups of calming hot tea, he led me to a chamber warmed by an old iron wood-burning stove. An arched window overlooked the courtyard and the dense snowfall that hung in the pines. Boots came off first, then sweater and pants, down to my thermals. I was too tired for the bowl of soup left on the bedside table. Once beneath layers of warm woolen blankets, deep sleep came swiftly.

*****

Sometime in the early morning light, half asleep, there came a vision. A whirlwind of snow danced around me then turned into red embers. The embers became pages of a book that fell to the floor. Words on the pages darted before my eyes, then a hot wind blew them away. It was one of those morning dreams, the kind I've had just before dawn when daylight gently pours over the night. Slowly, bright sunlight filtered in around my numbed senses. Drifting into consciousness, my deep slumber slipped away.

Yawning, I gently pulled aside the warm blankets. My bare feet touched the cold wooden floor. I was carried toward the light beaming in through the arched east window. Peering through frosted glass, I saw the most glorious sight my eyes had ever witnessed. The storm had passed, leaving only a few puffy white clouds that touched distant peaks. Golden sunlight crowned an alpine summit. Far-flung mountain ranges covered in virgin snow spread out before the valley below, where a quaint village came to life. Chimney smoke drifted, and brown Holsteins made trails through a snow-white pasture.

Raising the casement latch, I opened the window and breathed in crisp, cool morning air. Sunlight had overwhelmed the shadows of my dreams just as the last clouds had cleared the sky. Standing in the chill, I could have gazed at the glorious scene for hours.

There came a gentle knock on the chamber door. As I shut the casement, a sweet female voice called out in English. "Father Conley?"

Another knock, this one a little louder. "Father Conley, the abbey has awakened. The godly rise with the sun. A morning meal will be ready in fifteen minutes."

I responded, "Thank you. God be with you on this glorious day," realizing for the first time the unseen voice seemed familiar. She sounded American.

During the night, the fire in the stove had died out. In the cold chamber, kneeling before a crucifix nailed high on the wall, I prayed, "Thank You for my safe arrival through the perilous night. Expose the dream so that I can understand Your meaning."

In a psychology class at Boston University, it was taught that dreams occurred in the deepest stage of REM sleep; emotions of love, fear, confusion, and compassion express themselves as abstract images. Just recognize the emotion and you can make sense of the dream. Images of pages catching fire, falling to the ground were as confusing as the feelings behind them. If those images had meaning, it was beyond my limited understanding. Who can tell the meaning of such a dream but the Almighty? I could only believe its significance would be revealed to me in His benevolent time and place.

For now, there was little time to ponder. I was hungry. The bowl of soup I'd been too tired to eat the night before was now sitting on a cold stove. Hurriedly, I dressed in my only black robe and priest's collar, taking one more look over the bright valley before I headed downstairs to the dining hall.

Over the years, I'd learned something of the monastery at Saint Benedict. Its first little church was built for travelers in the Middle Ages by Benedictine monks. The rich and poor walked to the sacred places from Switzerland to Rome. They came to pray before relics of the saints taken from Jerusalem by the Crusaders. Here, a sliver of the crucifixion cross was preserved in glass. By following the pilgrim trail to the monastery at the top of the Alps, they found generosity and friendliness. For this traveler, refuge was no less than that of so many that had sought it in countless blizzards. Certainly no more than the pilgrims who had journeyed there for spiritual purity.

I ran down three flights of stairs and scooted in among the monks seated at a long table. Eagerly, I blurted out, "Good morning, everyone!" I received no response other than a disapproving look from more than one monk. My embarrassed, "Oh!" was the last word spoken. After that, a light breakfast of yogurt, grains, and blueberries in a ritual of silence as the practice of cloistered monks dictated.

When they had eaten, the monks prayed for a good while. Then one by one, in Gregorian chant, they filed out of the hall. It was magnificent. They say glaciers move faster than Catholic doctrine. Benedictines are seemingly more pious than modern American priests. I wanted to know more about the old traditions at the abbey. I also wanted to make sure the road was clear of ice, so I delayed my journey for at least a day.

A monk walked me to the office of the director, Monsignor Romano, a hard-worn, dedicated Benedictine monk. Formally, he greeted my arrival, "Che Dio sia con te" (May God be with you).

With deference, I responded, "And with you, Monsignor."

He looked at me like a parent looks at a son in trouble. "While in the abbey, among the monks, I must insist that you adhere to our strict rules of silence. However, these reservations are eased outside the abbey."

"Yes, Monsignor."

"What was the reason for your hasty journey to Saint Benedict?"

"On a mission from the Vatican to Heidelberg."

He drew closer to stress a point. "Nature is often unforgiving at these altitudes. Many have not survived the perilous journey during winter storms. We would not want to find another traveler at the bottom of a gorge!"

"I was impulsive and should have known better, Monsignor."

"Then your task is an important one?"

"Yes, vital to the church of Sant' Ambrogio."

"We will pray for the good of your church, Father Conley."

"*Grazie*, Monsignor. For the way ahead, many prayers will be needed."

"For us all. We live in a house of prayer."

"Monsignor, in your library…could you recommend an enlightening volume on the history of the abbey? I only know that Saint Benedict established guidelines for how the life of a monk should be lived."

"We do have a modest library, but here on these shelves are handwritten treatises from the seventh century." He turned to the wall of books behind his desk and scanned through the volumes. He picked out one ancient-looking leather-bound book. "Here is a hand-scribed copy of Saint Benedict's memoir. It tells of a hermit who lived in a cave gave his life to God."

Before handing the thick book to me, he paused. "These volumes must not be taken outside the abbey under any circumstances." He needed an affirmative response before releasing it into my hands.

Astonished at the fact that such a valuable artifact should be handed into my humble custody, I said, "On my sacred honor, it will be protected."

As our discord had been resolved, the mood brightened. "Father Conley, our monastery is, of many parts, a school, hospital, and more. A tour of the monastery has been arranged for you outside the abbey." When I assured him that I would like a tour very much, he said, "Normally, these things are carried out by a monk. However, we have an American, Dr. George, who volunteers at our clinic."

His attention turned to a stack of papers neatly weighted on his desk. So with that, our conversation seemed to have been completed. He looked up at me once more and finished. "I hope you find your stay at Saint Benedict inspirational. God go with you."

*****

To the east of the abbey, there was the pasture and dairy where monks there were at work early; to the west of the compound, across the open space, the medical clinic. Up the hill, in the morning sun, a bell chimed at All Saints' Academy. A sister summoned cheerful children of an Italian-Swiss village.

I walked the melting snow to the school door and slowly opened it. Standing near a front desk was a Franciscan nun who seemed to be taking instructions from one who, I assumed, was an administrator. It was the mysterious American woman. It could only be the one who had advised me that the abbey had awakened.

The nurse cued her with a silent glance that someone had entered the door behind her. And when, for the first time, she turned in my direction, I will confess in this memoir, even a priest will be attracted to a beautiful woman. Her name was Dr. Frances George. She was friendly and disarming, and the more I spoke to her, the more I became intrigued.

With a luminous smile, she greeted me. "Father Conley, welcome to our mission. I trust you had a peaceful sleep after your harrowing adventure driving up?"

Something about her eyes was strangely familiar, as if we had we known each other in some far-off place. Even the sound of her voice was mysteriously comforting. "Yes. So it was you that tapped on my chamber door this morning."

"We don't get many Americans at this secluded monastery. Glad you made it."

Gazing deep into those ocean-blue eyes, I murmured, "Glad I made it too."

She sensed my confusion, which was in no way unfamiliar to her concerning other men charmed with her presence. I told myself to snap out of it. A change of subject was in order. She said, "My dear Father Conley, would you like a tour of the academy?"

I must admit being relieved by the suggestion. "Thank you, Dr. George."

She led us through a yellow hallway, through the colonnade and around the courtyard, through sloshy, melting snow.

"Dr. George—"

"Doctor is so formal. Could you call me Frances?"

"Yes, of course. Frances, I have so many questions. You're a volunteer. How'd you choose this secluded sanctuary?"

"Well, I am not of an order of nuns. My parents married while attending an Oklahoma bible college. They became missionaries in India, the Philippines, and Amsterdam. My grandparents were wealthy bankers. By the time I was twelve, I could speak five languages. I earned a master's in child psychology at UCLA. My life will always be about helping the poor.

"For the time being, I am very happy here, teaching the enchanted children of the charming village of Alpha. So here I am. Would you like to meet them now? They have been excited to see you."

She guided me to a classroom with crayon-colored paper cut-outs on the walls, math equations scribbled on the chalkboard, and an incredible mountain view. A class of young students from ages, I'm guessing, ten to eighteen all in one room.

Frances introduced me to the class, "Sister Hensel, children, this is Father Conley. He has come a long way. Let's show him he is welcome at the academy."

All the children, smiling enthusiastically, responded. "*Buongiorno*, Father Conley!" Some giggled as I smiled back.

"*Buongiorno*. Good morning, kids!"

"The father has traveled all the way from America."

Oohs and ahs erupted from the little ones, and looks of admiration from the older ones prompted me to speak. "It's very nice to see you on this beautiful day. Tell me, who wants to say what your favorite subject is?"

A little girl with a pink ribbon in her hair raised her hand and proudly said, "History. We like history."

"And what has Sister Hensel taught you about history?"

A teenage boy dressed in a hand-sewn, embroidered smock stood up. "My name is Alex. I liked when Hannibal crossed the Alps to fight the Romans."

Hannibal, the Romans, I thought. *But that shouldn't be surprising. History was all around them. They are not like American kids who know really very little about the subject.* "Very good. And what would you like to know about America?"

The girls were interested in schools in America; the boys, sports. After almost an hour, I had to say, "You are all very fine students. Thank you for inviting me to your class. Would it be all right if I see you again?"

They all applauded the idea. I've always gotten along with children. It is bittersweet, of course, for I could never have any of my own. Dr. George and I thanked Sister Hensel and said good-bye to the children.

The children—laughing, giggling, waving their arms, and showing off just a little—responded in many languages. "*Arrivederci. Auf Wiedersehen. Au revoir.* Goodbye. Goodbye, Father Conley!"

We walked up the hill to the Benedictine's peacefully quiet clinic. A Catholic nurse attended an elderly woman in hospice care. Her family was around her. She sat up on her pillows with grandchildren on her bed. "Nena, can we see you tomorrow?"

"I will always be with you, darlings."

Her daughter burst into soft tears. I held her hand as we prayed for her salvation. The dying woman's eyes were overcome with gratitude and confidence in her everlasting life.

We were all overcome with emotion, but after some eternity, Frances and I again found ourselves walking in the brisk morning air. Frances solemnly said, "Few people of the mountain ever travel far from Alpha. They are born here, they live here, and they pass here."

"Many a city dweller wished they could have lived in a small village at the top of a mountain, though few ever do," I replied.

She said, "Let's go away from here. I'd like to show you the way they make cheese at Saint Benedict. I think you will enjoy it very much." With that, we strolled under a clear sky filled with the joyous sound of birds through the pasture to the old creamery.

Hibernica vine wrapped around its stone walls as lichen stained its gray slate roof. It was then she asked, "I've heard talk of your journey. Father John, are you on a mission from the Vatican? Is it true?"

"It may be only a vain search for the truth but one that may bring a church back to life and reassure an old woman, although I think Signora Campinella has lived in faith for her entire life."

"Truth comes in many ways, John. How will you look for it?"

"The signora told me that truth is hidden behind a dark veil, and I must unveil it. I'm sorry, but I don't want to sound so mysterious. It's just about a very special painting that's been missing for a long time."

She gave me that puzzled look that I've gotten used to over the years. "A painting?"

"And a priest, who also went missing. If the painting can be recovered—"

Then she said something that has encouraged me to this day. "Father, no one knows how, but if your intentions are pure, it will happen. When you find it, you may see God has led you all the way."

*****

There were four or five monks in the pungent-sweet creamery, all busy making cheese. A heated vat of milk was being stirred by hand. Screened cream was then poured into round forms and pressed. Another monk dusted and turned cheese rounds on shelves, where they would age for at least twelve years. According to their traditions and methods, the monks worked in silence.

Frances explained, "The creamery is actually older than the abbey. They have been making the same Alpen cheese since 1562. Every cheese is different. It's like fine wine. The flowers and herbs the cows eat are in the flavor of the cheese."

There was a table with a knife and cheese. She playfully put a small slice to my mouth. "Here, try."

As she had explained the goings-on at the school, talking about the children, her smile was comforting, her laugh contagious. Yet all the while, I couldn't help thinking I'd soon be on the way to Germany, not knowing what I might find.

She said, "I'm sure you have to get your things together for your journey, and I have to get back to the academy. It's been a wonderful morning. Perhaps I'll see you before you go."

I replied, "I plan to be on the road at dawn. If I don't see you, it's possible I can stop in on my way back to Rome."

She warmly said, "If God wills it, I will be interested in what you have found there." She touched my hand, and it was too obvious she felt a fondness for me. "Well, I guess it's goodbye for now. You will have a safe journey. I will pray it is so."

On the way back to the abbey, I thought about her. If I had met Frances before taking my vows to the church, it might have been different. In life, our choices shape our destiny. I had hoped in some way she would always be an influence in my life.

I returned to my sparse chamber before the sun sank behind the mountain sky. Looking forward to taking the road through Switzerland, I lit a fire in the stove to heat some black tea. I spent an hour pouring over my map, planning the next leg of the journey. Snow had been cleared by now, so it would be an easy road down from the summit. Lucerne, Switzerland might be a good place for respite. I marked the route in red. Many thoughts ran through my mind.

I had not opened the book on Saint Benedict. To my surprise, this was not a memoir from the saint himself. The accounts of his life were a compilation of writings inked by his monks after his death. In the year 500, near the end of the Middle Ages, he was sent to Rome. The accounts were of a young scholar who rejected the shameless lives of his fellow students. Benedict left the city to become a hermit.

He wrote his rules for living a Christian life, how to be humble, how to manage a monastery, and the rule of *ora et labora*, or how monks should work and pray. He died of fever in his abbey at Monte Casino, which was destroyed by Allied bombs in 1944. One more thing caught my attention: in his youth he was deeply affected by the love of a woman.

At an early hour sleep had not come as troubled thoughts still crowded my mind. A golden winter moon had risen. Its light streamed onto my bed like a beacon. I was compelled to unlatch and open the arched window. A soft, soothing breeze floated in the scent of evergreens as a billion points of light flickered in the ageless night. *Only God is eternal.* Falling to my knees, I prayed, "Lord, You told me at the altar of Sant' Ambrogio, that You would be there to guide me. Tell me what to say. Show me where to go. As I am blind, help me see the way."

Frances had reminded me of that. She was so full of life. Was I entranced by her? Not wanting to become a hermit, I prayed for chastity. "Judge me not for my weakness but for my devotion. Amen." My speculations fatefully drifted into a restful sleep.

Awaking to the predawn coo of mourning doves, a few things were quickly stuffed into on old rucksack. The monks' humble chant echoed from somewhere deep in the abbey. I made my way out to the carriage house without notice.

The Fiat had been washed, filled with gas, and readied for the long road ahead. A cotton bag on the passenger side was filled with bread, fresh fruit, and a wrapped slice of aromatic cheese. A handwritten note was pinned to the top. It read: "The children worried you wouldn't have enough to eat. They made this for your long journey. Be safe, Frances."

Under a dawning sky, the car rolled down the hill to the old pilgrim road. A few clouds caught the orange glow of sunrise. It would be a beautiful, clear day. Where the road would take was yet unknown. I was more than ready for it. At the bottom of the hill, the Fiat turned north to Switzerland.

Over the Alps

With the steady sound of the tiny puttering rear engine, dim yellow headlamps lit the way. It felt good to glide through the forest down from the summit. Childhood memories brought me back to fall's lush colors, riding in my dad's Ford on the back roads of Maine. The open road came with no introspections, no expectations. Dawn slowly faded some remaining eastern stars. Suddenly, welcome sunlight ignited the clouds and overtook the shadows in the peaceful low valleys. The car moved past green meadows with milk cows meandering along well-worn trails. Emerald lakes and shimmering streams emerged from the darkness.

As the sun climbed higher, I turned off the heater under the dash, switched off the headlights, and cranked open the driver's window to the sound of excited larks and finches. I pulled over at the side of a mountain brook, bent down to a clear stream, cupped my hands, and took a drink from energizing glacial waters. Looking up high, cloaked in white mist, mountain peaks appeared in the sky. Silvery waterfalls tumbled and sprayed below shear rock precipices. I wanted to climb every mountain.

The border crossing into Switzerland was anticlimactic. The car simply coasted over a rocky ridge. On a narrow mountain pass, there was a small sign on the side of the road. As it came closer, it grew larger till the colors became clear red and white. It was a painted Swiss flag. There were no guards, no gate, no passport required. I was in Switzerland.

Some days are golden. Snow from the early winter storm a few days before still lay on the ground in patches. The sun was just warm enough to counter the chill. At those altitudes, breathing in clean, thin air lifted my spirits. This was my first time in the Alps. Like that first day, on a clear crisp morning, or crimson sunset, my mind calmly melted into its placid peaks and verdant meadows.

At midmorning, I passed by a colorful gingerbread cottage. A farm family on a steep hillside was raking off hay to be carted to their barn before the looming winter set in. Such a simple life. A lot of work, but I could see myself living it.

Andermatt

At this point, I was purely an American tourist on an adventure. Up ahead, nestled among snow-covered peaks, came the loveliest medieval village made of colorful residential shops with pale-green shutters and steep roofs. I could have used a cup of hot chocolate, so when coming to it, I decided to stop at a quaint red café.

The proprietor was a robust gal with a dyed orange streak in her hair. Not wearing my priestly garb, except white collar under a windbreaker, she did not, at first, recognize me as a man of the cloth. And that was okay. In a friendly tone, she asked, "Guten morgen, ich habe hich nicht gesehen?"

My German was almost nonexistent. I politely asked, "Do you speak English?

"*Sprechen* English? English? You are English? *Ja, ja,* I can speak English." Now her friendly nature burst through in an enormous smile. She grabbed my hand and shook it for what seemed over a minute. "My name is Greta, Gre-ta. I was asking if you have been here before to our village, and good morning to you, Mister…?"

"It's a pleasure meeting you, Gre-ta. Call me John."

"Are you an American?" She seemed pleased that I was an American.

"I'm a little embarrassed to ask. My map is…where am I?"

She proudly announced, "We are in the wonderful village of Andermatt, and this is my little bakery *Die Kleine Backerei*. I have fresh scones, nut breads, and cakes. Would you like something?"

A woodburning heater in the corner was keeping the shop warm. I unzipped my windbreaker, unintentionally exposing the white collar. "You know, I was hoping for a cup of hot chocolate. Do you have hot chocolate?"

"Do I have chocolate? Do I have hot chocolate? Only the best, Father! All the way from Belgium it comes!"

At a cozy window table, I was in no hurry to get back in the car. The day was young, so I decided to linger at Greta's bakery. After a while, she brought large cup of hot chocolate, heaped with whipped cream, chocolate shavings floated on top, and a blueberry scone. She placed the cup on the table with a smile as warm as the chocolate. "I think you might like one of my scones. Have one. It's a gift, nothing extra."

"*Danke. Danke*, Greta." Looking over the scone, I exclaimed, "Are those blueberries? They're huge! Where do you find them?"

"Oh…along the streams, around the lakes."

"You make me feel at home, Greta. We have blueberries at home kind of like these."

With my eager approval, she pulled out a chair to sit across the table. "Father John, from where are you from in America?"

"A little town in Maine. You've probably never heard of. Waterville? Have you ever wanted to go to America?"

The way she responded shouldn't have surprised me, "I have…uh, thinked. Is that right?"

"Do you mean you thought about it?"

"Yes, I thought about it." She shook her head. "No, not really. I love my Andermatt. Wherever I may go, I could not take it with me."

"You are wise, Greta, wiser than most."

"Father John, where do you go from here?"

"On my way to Heidelberg."

"Is it for the church you are going?"

"It has something to do with the church, but today, I want to see your beautiful country. I want to drive through your valleys and forget why I'm going."

She seemed to see right through me but said nothing.

The bell over the door jingled as a young couple walked in. Greta excused herself, saying, "Father John, please wait for a moment. I have something for you." She walked over. Warmly greeted and took the couple's order. She returned unfolding a map of Switzerland. "May I suggest a route for you?"

"You are very helpful, Greta. Thank you so much."

With a pen, she traced a route familiar to her. "You will travel north through the Alps. You will pass the high peak of Oberalpstock, along the coast of Lake Nidwalden. You can stop in Lucerne if you like. The highway going north will take you over many rivers through many beautiful valleys. Mount Ruchen will be on your left. By taking your time to enjoy your journey, you can be on the Rhine by sunset."

"What a great map, Greta, very detailed."

"Father John, I know you could travel much farther tonight, but there is someone I think you should meet." She circled a village on the Rhine. "In the village of Basel lives Friar Geller. He is a man of many virtues. I don't know why, but as soon as you told me your journey had something to do with the church, I knew you should to speak to him."

But she couldn't know my mission, could she? No, she couldn't know. She just thinks I should meet him. That's all. "Greta, yes, I would like to meet your Friar."

"At the old Chateau Hofstetter in Basel. He is wise, some say the wisest man in all Switzerland or Bavaria. He is known by many in Germany."

I knew then that Greta's instincts told her that I was looking for something. How she knew it was as mysterious as her implication I contact the friar. "Yes, I want to meet Friar Geller. There is only one way to thank you, Greta." With an old monks prayer, I stood with her. "May faith be rising, faith lift your soul, a fresh new gift each day. May love be flowing, love bless your life, always cherished and ever safe. May Christ be your guiding light. Amen."

She responded, "And may God be with you."

We warmly said goodbye. I was not a big hugger, but she was, and I didn't mind. The bell over the door rang as a woman wearing a straw hat and coveralls came in. Greta greeted her as a friend.

I could have lingered a little longer in Andermatt but felt bound to get going. I thought it best to take Greta's route to Basel. There'd be a lot to see on her route to the Rhine. I planned to stop to marvel at even more astounding natural beauty on the way.

The Fiat's eager engine revved with the switch of the key. The battery was good, the gas tank more than half full. I pulled away from the curb and slowly cruised forward. The only way through Andermatt was Fraunhofer Lane, which was only about a half mile long leading back to the highway.

The village was lined with shops. They were open but only when someone walked in. Then the keeper would come forward from a back room or the apartment above to help a familiar customer. There were few people out on the street. I stopped to let a family with three children cross the lane to file into a bread shop. Such a small, contented village. I was naturally impressed with its serine beauty, like a ceramic alpine village under a Christmas tree.

Passing no stop signs or crosswalks, I picked up speed at the end of town. Now that I had a map and a plan, I was inspired and a little excited on a beautiful day, but I did not intend to exactly follow it.

In my family's tradition we always named our cars. This car needed a name. I thought, *It needs a name that means trustworthy and reliable. Kind of reminds me of* The Little Engine That Could *children's story, the amazing train that carried toys over the mountain. Let's see, the little engine in Italian is something like Piccolo Motore. That's it! From now on, the little Fiat will be Piccolo Motore!*

Now, I was on my way with the fervor of the little engine. Greta had said I'd cross many rivers. Far ahead was a big rocky mountain capped in white. *That must be Oberalpstock. There must be an incredible sunset view up there.*

Adjacent to the streams that flowed from the mighty glaciers, the road wound its way north past farms in small villages. I kept moving, Lucerne being my midday destination. The plan was to stop for lunch and top off the gas tank.

I took a breather at Lake Nidwalden, watching a few small boats cruise the glassy blue-green waters. If I only had brought my rod and reel! I could have spent the whole day fishing, sitting lazily on the shoreline under an aspen tree. But it was 11:00 a.m., and I was not yet at Mount Rucker.

The Little Engine rolled into Lucerne, a delightful place, beautifully painted buildings and a wooden walking bridge over the river. Trains and buses brought sightseers from all over the world. French, Chinese, Spanish, and Americans enjoyed a loitering lunch at a quayside café. In a bright, friendly atmosphere, they turned their heads to see children tossing bread crumbs to swans on the lake.

I was seated at a table by a busy waiter. "I'm Jorum. I'll be your server today. Would you like to try our *Buendner Pizokel* today? It's a hearty cheese fondue." He handed me an expensive menu that was steep for my frugal allotment of lira from the church. "Let's see. I'll just have a bowl of potato soup and some herbal tea."

As he walked away, I could almost hear him thinking, *Must not pay priests much in the Catholic church.* He was right, but if a priest were frugal, it was enough to get by.

I heard a familiar sound and looked behind to see a blue and white Chevy van drive into the piazza, loudspeakers blaring the Beatles song "Hey Jude." It was filled with American tourists, middle-aged women driven by a young long-haired male tour guide. They parked along the river near the bridge and tumbled out talking, laughing, having the time of their lives. They caused some small disturbance without a care in the world.

I heard someone on the next table scoff, "Americans! They think they own everything." I smiled and wondered what it must have been like driving that bus under different circumstances in another life.

*****

There was a Jesuit church in Lucerne in the Baroque style. I spoke to a young padre as the tourists whispered and snapped pictures of the skull of John the Baptist, which was allegedly its holy relic. "Crusaders brought many relics to the churches of Europe," said the padre.

"Yes, and these are fascinating!"

"Sometimes…the people need proof of their faith."

"Believe me, I understand that."

"Amen," he affirmed.

"Amen," I reaffirmed.

Our conversation served to be a reminder of *Santa Maria*. If the skull of John the Baptist had been lost, much of the spirit of this church would also be lost. But the painting of *Santa Maria* was not a relic. It could be returned to the church of Sant' Ambrogio.

*****

As long shadows crept up the courtyard walls, the little engine returned to the highway. Farther north, the sun inched down to the horizon as its inflamed light touched the tips of the distant peaks. I turned off on a gravel road that curved up to an Oberalpstock lookout and raced the sun, jogging the last hundred meters before it began to melt below the horizon. Just making what cannot be clearly described in words as just an awesome panoramic splash of color. And there was a mirage in the fading light probably caused by a lack of oxygen from running up the hill.

In the setting sun, Sant' Ambrogio appeared to be in flames. What if the vision were real? Had the vision come to say my church would burn? What then was my mission?

Watching from the top of the mountain, the apparition sank into the darkness. A cool breeze turned colder. Feeling insignificant under the timeless stars, my prayer for insight somewhat comforted my spirit.

Chateau Hofstetter

At last, I returned to the car, and it rolled down the gravel road to the moon lit highway. I arrived at the Chateau Hofstetter, once the estate of a duke or baron, not knowing exactly who Friar Gelder was or what his connection was with the château. But it felt right driving through the ornate iron gate on the way up to the manor.

The gardens around the courtyard were well kept. I parked the car and walked up several granite steps to a thick oak door engraved with an old family crest. An older man of rough refinement opened the grand foyer. He took my coat, saying, "Welcome, pilgrim. I am Macovescu. Have you come to speak with the friar?"

"I only hoped I could."

He asked me to wait in an adjoining sitting room. I could not help noticing plush surroundings. A grand staircase curved high up to the balcony on the second floor. The walls were cherry wood paneled. There was a colorful tile mosaic of an alpine meadow inlaid in the floor. The furniture was fourteenth century Bavarian. When he returned, he asked me to follow him to the chapel. "Friar Gelder is in meditation. You are welcome to join him in silence."

My intriguing guide led me through a long hallway to another wing and the stained glass door to the chapel. Kneeling before an altar adorned with a marble sculpture of Mary holding her holy child, was Friar Gelder. Not wishing to disturb him, I knelt close to the door. At once, I noticed a soft, pure light emanating from his body. As he prayed, his spirit seemed to illuminate the candled chapel. It was the strangest thing…I felt his spirit pass right through.

As he finally made the sign of the cross, I looked into his eyes. I'd never seen or been in the presence of such positive charisma. I reached for my crucifix and held it with both hands. "Welcome, young man."

"I'm Father Conley."

"Why have to come to this old château?"

"People say you are enlightened."

"And are you searching for a truth?"

"Yes."

"Father Conley, what did you see in your vision in the sun?"

Mystified, perplexed, bewildered for a moment, I tried to explain, "An old woman, Signora Campinella, had a vision that her church would be redeemed. I saw her church burning in the sun."

"And what do you believe?"

"That what I saw in the sun was a mirage, and what is possible is known in heaven."

"And yet you have never seen heaven!"

The friar came close and reached out his hand. With a gentle touch to my forehead, I was suddenly sent into a dream or trance. I was in deep space. It was me, but I was in the form of a featureless, luminous blue light, floating or flying among a billion stars. In the distance ahead, there was more blue light.

As I moved closer, I saw that it was not a single blue light but thousands of individual blue light spirits gathering together in a luminous sphere, one luminous spiritual orb. I whooshed into it as the warmest feeling I've ever felt enveloped me. More than the feeling of home I had as a child, more than a Christmas around the fireplace with family—one with the universe. In a moment, a flash of white light blinded my consciousness and I found myself again in the dim chapel.

Friar Gelder said, "Those in darkness shun the light. They are afraid of it. But if you believe in the light, live your life as if it has not been written in the stars. What is good in your heart brings good to you. Have faith in that!"

"I believe God has a plan for us all," I replied.

"There is the paradox. As you complete your own story, you may come to realize it was preordained before the mountains rose."

Macovescu appeared at the door. The friar, with both hands, held mine. "I will keep you in my prayers, young seeker. I must leave you to make ready for a journey tomorrow. You are tired and hungry. Macovescu will make your stay comfortable."

While sitting at a marble counter in the large kitchen, I began to notice the regal château had become a monastery, bare of its once-elaborate furnishings and dimly lit with only a few tall candles. Macovescu seemed a man of few words. "This is *palacsinta*. It is Hungarian crepes."

"Sir, do you mind if I ask, how you know the friar? How did you first meet him?"

His head nodded affirmatively. "It was during the war in Romania. I was a boxer who joined the Severin resistance, fighting Nazis. For weeks I hid from the gestapo, barn to attic. My days were surely numbered. It was Friar Gelder who saved my life, like he saved many others. You see, he had organized an underground that smuggled Jews into Switzerland. I was just one more soul he saved. I am the servant and protector of an extraordinary man."

Macovescu showed me a simple chamber where I was to stay the night. My spartan surroundings consisted of a single bed, a chest of drawers, and on a stand, one flickering candle. On the wall hung a carved wooden cross. It had been a long, enlightening day. I could not yet comprehend the wisdom in the blue light.

Overwhelmed, I only wanted to unwind and relax, maybe read a book. The book! No! *The book!* With a flurry, I opened my old rucksack, which was lying on the bed. My hand fished deep inside among my clothes. It felt something that I hoped it was not. I pulled it out, but it was. Early that morning, in haste, I had inadvertently stowed Saint Benedict's Memoirs, the manuscript Monsignor Romano had directly said was never to leave the Benedictine Abbey.

Mortified, I scolded myself, *I'll have to face him.* I thought that it may not be a bad idea to stop by the monastery anyway. I wrapped the book in the map of Switzerland and stuffed it back in the sack.

Changing into a night shirt, I found my way to the chapel to meditate and pray on my revelations. On my return to the bed chamber, there was a curious letter that had been slipped under the door.

Father Conley,

There is a man in West Berlin, Pastor Braun. He resides at the church of St. Pius. He has found many lost arts. Perhaps he can guide you to your Saint Mary. You may present him with this letter of recommendation.

May what you seek be drawn to you,

Friar Gelder

Secrets behind the Wall

At earliest light, the North Star faded into a pastel blue sky. In Basel, I crossed over the river Rhine. Germany was not Italy. The border police were alert and focused on the smallest details. I waited in the queue while they practically tore apart any suspicious traveler's car. When my time came, an intimidating guard explained that mine would be only a cursory inspection. He said, "Yes, an inconvenience, but there is a cold war on!" Otherwise, there was little problem getting into *Deutschland*.

Once through the crossing and after rearranging the back seat, I gladly revved the engine and drove away feeling liberated. It would be a nine- or ten-hour drive to Berlin, even taking the autobahn. BMWs and Mercedes-Benzes streaked by at 110 while the old Fiat barely made sixty miles an hour.

Of course, I stayed in the *slow* lane as they sped past. *Well, Piccolo Motore may not be a Beemer, but she'll get me there.* The little engine had plenty to be proud of. It had climbed many a challenging Alpine summit. I was fairly confident that with some prayer, my little car would get me back to Florence.

I drove past miles of low stubbled winter wheat fields and what remained of row crops. Through green forests and bare vineyards that called me to rest, I kept driving. For the most part, I kept to the autobahn, which skirted Stuttgart. Once or twice I turned off what seemed the endless autobahn into a small village for petrol. Macovescu had packed a paperboard box with some of his delectable Romanian pastries. I sat on the quiet park bench to review the map.

Being in a hurry to get to Berlin, it was not long before I drove back to the main road. I would have liked to explore Nuremburg, but the sightseeing as enjoyed in Switzerland would have to wait. A few hours more and Leipzig served as a landmark not far from Berlin.

The German people were amazing. For one thing, they had rebuilt their severely war-damaged cities in less than thirty years. No longer were there bombed out buildings as seen in other places but new, modern ones and beautifully restored medieval ones.

The ten hours did not go by swiftly. It was a long ride. Friar Gelder's wisdom lingered the whole time. I still believed restoring the church was in God's plan, but I knew now more than ever, I'd have to do the uncovering. It was not an either-or proposition; it was both. These thoughts assured me in unfamiliar places where the friar's counsel became clear and meaningful.

Germany was still divided East and West during the Cold War. The Soviet Union had gripped the East, the West had become a free democratic country. A barbed-wire-guarded wall, built by the Soviets, divided its people. Once through a gate, it was a two-hour drive through a narrow corridor to get to West Berlin. Guards passed me through after only twenty minutes, scrutinizing my identification. Again, I felt the efficiency and rules that Germans live by.

The Berlin skyline began to appear about 4:00 p.m. West Berlin was beautiful, lively, and clean—no litter, no graffiti. The spires of St. Pius were easily visible. Without delay, I drove directly to them. A low-toned church bell rang somewhere as the engine shut down in a visitors' parking lot. I began to realize I was in a city where Lutheran churches outnumbered Catholic ten to one. St. Pius is a much taller church than Sant' Ambrogio, though not as old. I sat in the rear pew to watch a wedding rehearsal and some enthusiastic tourists who took pictures.

Pastor Braun had a cool nerve and an adventurous soul. When he read Friar Gelder's letter, he greeted me as a compatriot. "Your reason for coming must be of importance to be recommended by the great man."

I responded, "I believe he saw more than he thought wise to tell me."

"I knew him when he led a peace mission in Bosnia building hospitals for the Red Cross. He is an unconventional traveling friar, who is always involved in exceptionally good things. But who can truly know Friar Gelder? Well, how can I help you, Father Conley?"

"The friar told me that you look for lost artworks. Have you heard of the painting taken from the church of Sant' Ambrogio? I've come to find it!"

What he said surprised me. "You are not the only one who has searched for Granacci's *Santa Maria*. In twenty-five years involved in German stolen artworks, it has eluded us."

"Have you found nothing of it?"

"Come with me, Father Conley, to our archives and the catalogs of lost and recovered arts, just to make sure."

In the library of St. Pius, we examined catalogs of lost arts that had once been the property of private citizens, churches, and museums. There were photographs of hundreds of artworks cataloged. He located the image of the *Santa Maria* but found nothing of its whereabouts. "We can only hope it may someday turn up in a private collection," Pastor Braun lamented.

The Vatican had time to wait. Sant' Ambrogio did not. "Has the organization given up on it?"

He claimed they hadn't, saying, "No, I don't believe so, but it's always a matter of resources. There are many others more promising to follow. We only know it was taken during the German retreat from Florence. Nothing more."

To the organization, our *Saint Mary* was not any longer a priority. Then I said, "Pastor Braun, I see the record does not mention a gestapo colonel by the name of Ziegler."

"Ziegler?"

"It is told on the streets of Florence, on the night the bridges were destroyed, the painting was taken by a Colonel Ziegler."

"What more have you heard? We need to know the whole story."

"Others were involved: the parish priest, Father Lombardi, known as a collaborator, and his cohort Captain Mueller. I was told by Father Bruno, who was told by others."

"Fantastic! Then we must try to locate this man."

"Pastor, what do you think the chances are we'll find him?"

"I will send out the word. There is a network of those actively searching for stolen art. Some, unsavory as they may be, deal in lost antiquities. And then there are the Nazi hunters who look for war criminals. I have to caution you. Many high-ranking German officers have fled to South America. After so many years, Ziegler may not still be alive."

I felt the odds stacking up on the wrong side. "But if they can try, I will pray. I will pray in your church day and night."

He said with a confident grin, "Like they say in America, it's a long shot. But do not be discouraged, Father Conley. We are German. We have a very efficient organization. With the grace of God, we will locate this man."

I added, "I will pray that he has accepted Christ."

*****

Over the next three days, Pastor Braun was not seen at St. Pius. I rightly assumed he was organizing a search. I spent my time in the church and rectory. I pored over the memoirs of Saint Benedict and mused, *Maybe the life of a sequestered monk would be better. Then again, not for my adventurist soul.*

On the third afternoon, someone knocked on the door. Pastor Braun looked excited. "There is good and bad news from a secondhand source."

"Give me the bad news first," I said.

"It is thought that Captain Mueller was killed in a bombing raid in Heidelberg."

I said, "That's unfortunate. I hoped we might have learned much from Father Lombardi's collaborator."

Pastor Braun continued. "However, Ziegler is living in East Berlin at the Hotel Rheinstadter! Even now, we are making clandestine plans to question him. It will be difficult. Only with the help of our organization might it take place. Are you willing to go to Soviet Berlin to find your painting?"

Excited, I responded, "Are you kidding? I'd be willing go through to the gates of Hades! It has to be tried. When do we leave?"

"We'll be going over tonight. The East German police will be very suspicious. They will want to know why we're going. Looking for artworks is one thing, but looking for a Nazi colonel is by far another. Friends will be watching after us, but we may also be followed by secret police. If the Stasi would find out we are looking for a Nazi, they would invent a reason to hold us. It's very dangerous. Some who have attempted it have vanished, never to be seen again."

That night, Pastor Braun drove a black Mercedes to the East Berlin gate. He said, "I've been through here before. They will want to know why we've come. There are spies everywhere. Let me do all the talking. If you are asked a question, respond with simplicity, or I will speak for you."

A heavily guarded gate barred the entrance to the eastern city. On a dark moonless night, we were stopped for inspection. Intense floodlights illuminated the eerie crossing. An upward beam stressed that the East German flag flew above the guardhouse. We stopped behind the blockade and were immediately surrounded by police and soldiers armed with automatic weapons.

A hard knock on the passenger side insisted I roll down the window. A flashlight probed the interior, trying to spot any contraband being smuggled in. It felt like entering a prison. I soon found it was not far from the truth. A guard of some rank loomed at the driver's side window. "I'll need to see identification."

Pastor Braun handed over our passports. He also had a diplomatic pass he had apparently used crossing the border on other occasions. The inspector took the papers and entered the guardhouse. After anxious minutes on my part, the guard came back and sternly insisted, "Pastor Braun, why visit East Berlin at this hour?"

The pastor answered with confidence. "To another art conference at the Veliger. The gallery is showing a Rembrandt tonight. I wouldn't want to miss it."

He then cast his suspicious eyes on me. "Who is this?"

Before I could speak, Pastor Braun interjected, "He's a young priest, only my assistant."

When the inspector had had enough of us, they lifted the bar, and we drove through. As we rolled out of the lights, I felt very relieved. A little confused traveling through the city, I asked, "Pastor Braun, are we going to an art gallery? I thought we were going—"

"Yes and no. We will see the Rembrandt only for a moment. When we get word it's safe, we will be driven to the hotel to see your Nazi. It's all been arranged, even the Rembrandt. They have their spies. We have ours."

"Amazing," I muttered.

So there I was in East Berlin. So young, so intrigued—I could hardly believe it. It was very surreal. On the way to our destination, I mentioned, "Contrary to what I've heard back in the States, in East Berlin, there are still some bombed-out buildings. Apparently, the city seems to have been mostly rebuilt."

He informed me, "We know they poured a lot into it, hoping to make it a showcase for their Communist doctrine. Unfortunately, it has fallen far behind the West."

Soon, we pulled up in front of the gallery. It had been well arranged, well advertised on short notice. It was as gala an affair as could happen in East Berlin at the time. The museum was well lit. Valets parked cars as the well-off, dressed in their finest, went in. In a reserved spot, Pastor Braun locked the car doors, saying, "Stay alert! Stay close!"

We walked in to be seen but not to be seen. The police, stationed outside, took note of those who came. The famous painting was being viewed in a separate gallery. I had recently seen the great art museums of Florence and Rome. Of course, my appreciation for the classic masterworks had increased. I stood in front of the Rembrandt, not forgetting why I was there.

While wishing to stay a little longer, there was a tap on my shoulder. A nod from Pastor Braun signaled we were ready to leave. Inconspicuously as possible, we were led into a private room, out a back door, and into a car driven by a mysterious man. We were taken to the old Hotel Rheinstadter. The pastor and I got out in the alley behind the hotel. The car crept away into the shadows.

We quietly climbed the iron fire escape up to the third floor. The old brick hotel, though not elegant even in its prime, was now being used as kind of a last refuge for dying old men. It was depressing, a place with filthy walls and the hallway had the lingering stench of urine.

We walked past a few forgotten souls languishing in wheelchairs. At last, we located the dark room where Colonel Ziegler was lying on his bed, hooked up on life support. A suspicious nurse discovered us in the room and hurriedly made her way down the hall and out of sight. Pastor Braun and I looked at each other, knowing we'd only have a few minutes to obtain any information we could get from the dying man.

The chart hanging at the end of his bed indicated, "HOSPICE." We came closer. The man was having trouble breathing. When I spoke his name, Ziegler raised an arm and pointed directly at me. I saw the desperate, frightened look in the eyes of a man dying without faith or redemption for things he had done. The old Nazi could not speak as he strained to say anything. Even if he had known the whereabouts of the *Santa Maria*, he was unable to say so. At this point, all we could do was give him absolution, whether he wanted it or not.

Just then, through the third-story window, came the sound of screeching brakes. Loud orders were given. Someone had been summoned. We had to get out quickly!

As we ran down the hallway, we heard a dozen heavy boots rushing up three flights of wooden stairs. It sounded like a herd of rogue elephants. We rushed down the fire escape to the car. The driver made a zigzag retreat through side streets and narrow alleys back to the gallery. We picked up the original car that took us to the gate, where we were lightly inspected and let go. Our pursuers arrived seconds later, only to watch us swiftly pass into West Berlin.

A Time for Repose

We returned from East Berlin with no clue as to whether the precious painting had even survived the war. Feeling overwhelmed and possibly coming down with a mild fever, I ambled directly to my room and crawled into bed. The last few days, the last week, had been stressful. I slept a long, restful sleep and did not awake until noon.

Thick clouds had darkened the sky. Icy rain pelted the roof. I took one look out of the window, just to bury my face in the pillow, once again unwilling to think about the painting or anything else, for that matter. Repose provided consolation for all that had been chanced.

A chill in the room worsened my symptoms. A mild headache, itchy sore throat, and being achy all over gave me a good reason to stay in bed. I reached over and grabbed a sweater, fluffed up the pillows, and opened the writings of Saint Benedict. That stormy Wednesday was spent snuggled under soft blankets, reading and napping. A nun brought a cup of hot tea and a bowl of soup to my bedside table. My mission was on hold. I was sure dealing with the consequences of recent events would come after a few days of rest and peace.

For the next few days, I immersed myself in reflection and prayer on the grounds of St. Pius.

My diary revealed my state of mind:

My whole effort to locate the painting seems to have come to an end. The last known surviving witness has died without disclosing its existence. The only thing left to do is write to Monsignor DeLuca at the Vatican. I have learned that there are many illusions in life. I will continue to believe the dark veil will be lifted in the end.

No matter how dire it seemed, I did not want to give up my mission and so delayed writing to Monsignor DeLuca.

*****

The sun came out on Saturday. I was feeling better, though melancholy. I made my way to the kitchen, where I savored a frosted German pastry and black coffee. It was warming up in the courtyard. I strolled on a cobblestone path through gardens covered with wet multicolored leaves. For a while, I rested on a bench encircled by autumn flowers. There, I reflected on Ecclesiastes. "There is a time and a season for all things under heaven. There is a time to lose and a time to gain."

Job was tested by God. All the faithful are eventually tested. I decided to remain vigilant for the sake of the people of Sant' Ambrogio.

The day remained cold, sunny, and somber. I washed and packed my clothes. Then refueled and checked the tires and oil in the Fiat for a journey yet unknown. Sunday morning would come early. I planned to be on the highway shortly after chapel prayer.

A little while later, not more than a block away was a farmers market where, with a few marks, I bought loaf of crusty bread, a slice of red Bavarian cheese, and a jar of strawberry jam. I stopped in a small café, sat at a corner table, and had a light supper while reading the West Berlin news. Returning to St. Pius feeling better, I went to see him but was told Pastor Braun was out of the city. I wrote my farewell, thanking him for all his assistance and left it on his desk.

An orange light waned in the western window. In a cold room, I eagerly slipped under the covers and picked up the book lying on the bedside table. The writings of Saint Benedict read, "All the darkness in the world cannot extinguish the light of a single candle."

As the eastern sky began to lighten, I rousted out of bed with a fresh, liberated attitude. If there was something bigger going on, it was something beyond me. I sang in the shower for the first time in weeks. As far as all the drama, I'd just let it go! I planned to take some time to enjoy the day in a nice café, read the funny papers, and explore the city.

I knelt beneath the crucifix for a simple morning prayer for serenity in whatever may come. When I opened the chamber door, there were familiar voices coming from the lobby. Curiosity carried me forward. I quickly reached the bottom of the stairs to see the mysterious driver rush out the door. It was the man who had spirited us through the back alleys of East Berlin. A light from the library caught my attention. Pastor Braun, was at his desk, reading my farewell note. "Father Conley, so you have not gone."

Cautiously, I replied, "No, not yet."

"The news I've anticipated has just now arrived. We need to talk!"

"What news? Has it come from the driver?"

"Yes, he has driven through the night from Heidelberg."

"Does this news have to do with the *Santa Maria*?"

Pastor Braun explained, "Two days ago, I suggested he go to Heidelberg to verify that the deceased Captain Mueller was indeed the same Mueller who collaborated with Father Lombardi."

Clutching my silver crucifix, I anxiously inquired, "Has he found how he was killed?"

"Well, no. Capt. Frederick Mueller is very much alive!"

I crossed myself and whispered, "The Lord is with us!"

Pastor Braun responded, "He is."

We knelt and prayed to complete our mission. Pastor Braun said, "It is likely he tells you nothing. I could ask the driver to go with you."

I remembered Rosalie Campinella, Friar Gelder, and the vow I took at the church of Sant' Ambrogio. It had been a roller-coaster ride. I reflected on all the ups and downs and reversals on the journey. My hopes, both dim and bright from dark dreams and refreshing dawns, challenged my resolve. I was optimistic, knowing Captain Mueller could propel the coaster to the truth. "Pastor Braun, I think I'll have to go it alone!"

"As you wish it, young pastor. But if he is belligerent and tells you nothing? It is difficult to see how you would be able to convince him to do the right thing. In that case, it could mean the end of our hopes."

Frederick Mueller

I was now on the way to Heidelberg, my original destination. Ironic how it all had gone full circle. Knowing very little about Mueller, I sensed that he held the vital key to my most positive expectations. All through with speculation, I would confront the old Nazi! I'd provoke him like an archangel in hell with an avenging sword of righteousness. These thoughts, although fanciful, increased my confidence for the inevitable clash.

Inspecting a map of Germany, I figured it would be a six-hour drive to my destination. In order to avoid the larger cities like Potsdam, I took the 115 South. About halfway, the route turned onto 19 Southwest. I drove on, stopping only once in the old city of Wurzburg to refuel and refresh myself. For the most part, the roads were not autobahn, but I made good time driving on narrow country highways. Midday, at the crest of a hill, I could see the Neckar River and the charming city of Heidelberg.

The place I was looking for was in an old-town pedestrian zone. I parked a block away and walked past restaurants and shops crowded with delighted sightseers, who spoke many languages. I was surprised to find that the old captain's art gallery was not in some dark hidden back alley but right in the center of a charming marketplace.

Just to make sure, Pastor Braun had written the address on a scrap of paper. I reached into my coat pocket. It was an expensive gallery at 324 Hauptstrasse, *Kunst der Welt* or Arts of the World. I took a deep breath, crossed the lane, and entered, causing a bell to jingle over the door.

It was a beautiful gallery filled with wonderful paintings and colorful ceramics. I had to admit, for a lover of arts, it was an exciting discovery. But I had no time for that. I first saw him standing at a table, unpacking a wooden crate. It was an exquisite vase. Inspecting it, he satisfactorily uttered, "Yuan Dynasty!"

I watched him awhile caress the vase. At first, he did not notice my presence. "Excuse me!" I said.

When the ceramic was carefully placed back in its shipping crate, he glanced my way and said, "Oh, I'm sorry. *Willkommen.* Welcome to my gallery."

He appeared to be in his early seventies, tall and fit. There was a racing bike at the back wall. He had a worldly, charismatic confidence that was wholly unexpected. I thought the old Nazi would be secretive and distrustful. His greeting took me completely off guard. The friendly approach wouldn't fool me. I wondered which of these artworks he had stolen.

"Father, we have some of the best artwork in Heidelberg. Is there something I can help you with?"

"What happened to Granacci's *Santa Maria*, Captain Mueller?"

"I see you know my name. Who are you to come into my shop to ask provocative questions?"

"My name is Conley, Father John Conley. I've come from a church in Florence. You might remember it. Sant'Ambrogio?"

"Yes, I remember it. I have remembered it for forty years."

"It is said in the markets of Florence that during the war, you had a collaborator. The people say that collaborator was the traitor Father Lombardi. You stole a valuable piece of art from the church, which has not been seen again. I've come to recover it."

What he said sent my mind reeling backward. "Traitor? Do you think Lombardi was a traitor? Let me tell you something about Father Lombardi. He was my friend. He possessed a love of art as I did. He was a great man of understanding and a dedicated priest. You know, he died for his church and for the people of Florence. Don't tell me he was a traitor!"

I shot back, "It is known on the night they bombed the bridges, you, Colonel Ziegler, and Lombardi took the painting from the church. Do you deny it?"

"I remember as if it were yesterday. It was a time of great turmoil. The war was coming to an end. I was aware he had been accused, but who would listen to a German officer trying to defend a collaborator priest?"

Both our moods calmed a little. I asked, "You say he died defending the church. How can you say Father Lombardi died for the church when he worked for the gestapo? I'm sorry, Herr Mueller, if I insulted you, but I have to know how he died."

A look of surrender came over Frederick Mueller. "I must go back in time, to Florence in 1944. Let me remember it well. I would like to tell you in my own words, from my perspective. Come with me where I gather my thoughts. I will tell you about Father Lombardi."

He took me back to a den heated by an ornate iron stove. An orderly desk was nestled in a corner. Bright watercolors crowded the walls, exotic pottery weighted every shelf and table. The stove centered around four comfortable overstuffed leather chairs. He invited me to sit near the fire then picked up a steaming kettle from the burner. "Do you like tea, Father Conley?"

"Thank you, Captain Mueller. *Danke.*"

He poured aromatic chamomile into two exquisite porcelain cups. "Please don't call me captain. The war has been over for years." Herr Mueller paced the floor and started his story. "It was hot in the city that night. Burning bridges filled the air with smoke. I was sure Father Lombardi would be in danger from the partisans. I made my way to the church of Sant' Ambrogio. The streets were dark and dangerous. I took a familiar circuitous route.

"When I arrived, the church was surrounded by German troops. A battle-hardened sergeant did not deny my entrance. Colonel Ziegler, may he burn in hell, was as angry as I had ever seen him. Father Lombardi was tied to a chair, slumped over with blood on his face. He was being interrogated, for what I could not imagine. When he became conscious, they continued to threaten him. I protested, but Ziegler was my superior officer, and there was nothing I could do!"

"What did they want to know?"

"They wanted to know where the Granacci was! Don't you see? When I arrived, the *Santa Maria* was not in its place on the wall." Mueller took a sip of tea.

"But how could that be? The doors had been watched by the gestapo that entire day."

"Yes, that is true. No one could have passed in or out of the church without being seen. Obviously, Colonel Ziegler thought Father Lombardi had hidden the painting somewhere in the sanctuary itself."

"That's impossible!" I insisted. "The walls are made of thick granite blocks, the floors heavy marble. If there were such a hiding place, Father Bruno would have known. As for myself, I have cleaned and swept every inch of the sanctuary. Herr Mueller, there is nowhere a painting of that size could have been concealed by one man or by many in so short a time."

Mueller responded, "That is odd. For these many years, I assumed it had been returned to its rightful place. A good man has been martyred for his devotion. Now you tell me the good father was libeled by his own people."

I couldn't blame him for feeling dismayed. I had bought into the rumors myself, not a very Christian thing to do. I questioned my own devotion, ashamed of what I had assumed about men I did not know. "Sir, I have offended you and brought up sad memories. For that, I am truly sorry. But I have to know. What happened after they took you and Father Lombardi away?"

Through with pacing the floor, Mueller rested in the leather chair by the stove. "After the firefight, they rushed us both out the back door and into Ziegler's staff car. Eight or nine of them followed us in a canvas-covered truck. We sped through the night, arriving in Berlin the next afternoon.

"At gestapo headquarters in a dingy basement cell, the interrogation continued as the bravest man I ever met prayed for strength. Ziegler momentarily left the room, and I knew I had just one chance to save his life. I begged my good friend, 'You don't have to do this! Give them what they want! Tell them! Save yourself!'

"I came close to him to hear his dry voice whisper its last words: 'In domo Christi.'"

I said, "My Latin isn't what it should be. Is it the house of Christ?"

"More precisely, in the house of Christ."

"It sounds like a riddle. Do you know what he was trying to tell you?"

"I had no reason to think there was a hidden message in it."

"Did he say anything else?"

"In his dying breath, he uttered the name Granacci."

A heavy cloud of melancholy drifted over the room. An upsetting memory was all that was left of Father Lombardi. Herr Mueller said, "I walked the streets of Berlin that night while wailing sirens mourned. What have we done?"

The story was complete. There was nothing more he could tell. We silently sat sipping tea. I glanced at him once or twice, wondering how often these dreams had invaded his sleep. The bell over the gallery door woke him from his dark memory.

Herr Mueller rose from his chair, placed the cup on the stove, and said, "I would like to speak more about Father Lombardi. I have an apartment above the shop. You are more than welcome to it."

I stepped away from the gallery doorway into the fresh autumn air. I shielded my eyes from the golden sunlight. I wanted to run, rejoice, greet people in the streets with the good news. I whistled my way to the center of the Marc Platz, wanting to shout out. A dark veil had been lifted; there was hope for everyone!

In old Europe, whether they called it a piazza or plaza, it was the same—a cobblestone marketplace surrounded by intriguing medieval window shops. A fountain with effigy offers a reflection into history. Would there be constructed an image of Father Lombardi in the center of Piazza Sant' Ambrogio?

I strolled past a bakery, cafés, and antique sellers. Students from the University of Heidelberg gathered around the fountain. At open-air cafés, sightseers sat at little round tables and tasted flutes of sweet Riesling under blue umbrellas. The west end of busy Marc Platz was dominated by the Lutheran Church of the Holy Spirit. It was almost empty at that hour.

I went in and sat in a pew, reflecting on what I'd just learned. I had seen in my thoughts a willingness to accept my suspicions without proof, no better than the people on the streets of Florence. How could I expect them see their folly if I had not seen my own?

In the warm afternoon, there were precious hours to explore the city. I crossed the Neckar River bridge and hiked up to Heidelberg Castle, stepping aside as bicycles raced down. At the top, granite stairs corkscrewed up a castle tower. I saw a panorama of fall-colored hills, with the river winding around then out of sight. And below, from near and far what people to see, the perfect postcard that is Heidelberg.

On the way back, a block from the expensive tourist area, a family-run *kaffeehaus* offered the special of the day. Bavarian sausage, cheese potatoes, and brussels sprouts were right for my modest pocket. By six o'clock, the sun was fading behind the hills. At that magic hour, it turned the old city amber and red. I eagerly revisited the gallery just before it closed for the day.

*****

Herr Mueller led me to the third-floor residence, where the walls were neatly arranged with his private collection of the most exquisite artwork. He opened the door to the room I'd be staying in, also occupied with rare watercolors and oils. The shutters were open.

I peered down to the *platz* where the tables were busy. I gazed beyond the rooftops at purple-gray landscapes. "Would you care for something to eat, Father Conley? I am somewhat a gastronome."

In this way, he continued to surprise my highest expectations of him. "No, thank you. I just had something."

He said, "I am not so hungry myself. Let's have some wine."

Mueller brought a bottle of Chianti to the kitchen table and, like an old soldier, removed the cork with a pocketknife. He poured the wine into two regular water glasses. He lifted his glass. "To Father Lombardi!"

"Yes, to Father Lombardi!"

We tapped our glasses. I fidgeted with my glass and watched him read the international arts news. Finally, I got up the courage to ask him what I'd been wondering. "Herr Mueller?"

He peered over his bifocals and politely responded, "What is it, Father Conley?"

"Regretfully, I had a different impression of you when I first stepped into your gallery. You are not who I expected. What I want to know is…how does an officer in the Third Reich prove to be a man of compassion?"

He folded the newspaper. "I come from an old aristocratic military family. Yes, I was a Nazi, no excuse for that, just an explanation if you indulge it. An officer was expected to be a party member.

"Before joining the *Wehrmacht*, I earned a master of arts in Zurich. With my family connections, I was posted to the diplomatic corps. Those were exciting times for Germany, and no one wanted to accept the possible consequences.

"In 1944, I was with the foreign ministry at the German consulate in Florence. There, I met Father Lombardi at the famous Uffizi Gallery. Both being amateur art historians, we soon formed a subtle friendship. When he showed me Granacci's *Santa Maria* hanging in his church, I thought it remarkable."

"How so?" I asked.

"Well, just that art of such value could be hanging undisturbed on a small local church wall for more than five hundred years. When the gestapo arrived, Italian partisans were rounded up and summarily shot! Since the war, I have not had a desire to return to Florence. I dedicated myself to the knowledge of the arts of the world."

"And has it taken you far, Herr Mueller?"

"To a temple in Kandahar, where I drank from a well of clear desert water. From there, I found other wells of knowledge to drink from Shanghai, Syria, Burma, Tibet. I've meditated on ancient scrolls of the Hindus, Buddhists, and Muslims."

"In Proverbs, it says, 'The ear of the wise seeketh knowledge.'"

"And," he said, "the heart of the prudent gaineth knowledge."

"Herr Mueller, are you a Christian?"

"The scriptures say that there is no wealth like knowledge and no poverty like ignorance."

"Is that Old Testament?" I asked.

"It was Buddha."

"Are you Buddhist?"

"I am a seeker."

"But only through Jesus can we know God."

"Yes." Mueller spoke slowly, "I will ask you what I ask many Christians. If a child is born on a secluded South Pacific island, where there has never been knowledge of the Bible, can he truly know God? Does God not exist on that island?"

"But you agreed that only through Jesus can we know God. Are you saying there are other ways?" I protested.

Herr Mueller reflected. "The light is the light. Man has always found himself living within a mysterious eternal world. He has gazed at the stars to seek a greater consciousness through faith. With little knowledge, people have tried to define the Holy Spirit by making icons."

"But Jesus came to save the world from primitive beliefs."

"Maybe so, but would the creator of love withhold salvation from an innocent child? No, I think not. I have seen otherwise in many faraway places."

At the time, I could only try to wrap my head around all he said. It was then, on that journey, I decided to know much more about the world, its history and the people in it.

Herr Mueller rose from his chair, opened a cabinet, and picked a small bronze icon. "What is it?" I asked.

"It represents a Syrian goddess." He brought it to the table where I could inspect the small image. "You see here, she is wearing a horned headdress. It is Astarte, goddess of love and war. Before 700 BC, she was as revered as Mary is today."

After I'd had a chance to examine it, he said, "Enough of artifacts. I have collected many of them from around the world. We will drink to history and to the gods."

We clinked glasses, but I drank only to the Savior.

"And what about you Father Conley, where were you born?"

"Oh, I'm just a farm boy from Maine."

"Maine? Let me tell you, I have never been."

"Yeah, near Bucksport," I said.

He was washing dishes at the sink when he turned around, saying, "It is good that you have come to open my memories of Father Lombardi." He dried his reddened hands with a dish towel. "I have not spoken of him to anyone in all these years."

We sat at the table and poured more wine. "Herr Mueller, what was it like when you knew him? Who was Father Lombardi?"

"All right. But…you have never seen war."

He looked up at the ceiling to gather his thoughts, "In the beginning, not many saw much in Hitler. You know, he was arrested and thrown into prison for trying to overturn the government. Hitler spoke to veterans and forgotten citizens who saw the dangers of the Soviet communists as they tried to infiltrate the fatherland. They blamed the betrayal on Jewish politicians. Germany was in trouble, and Herr Hitler seemed to have the answers people wanted to hear. With the rallies, parades, and a newfound pride, it was as though we'd found our new Frederick the Great! I have to admit, I was carried along with the enthusiasm.

"Of course, it didn't last long. In the foreign ministry, I saw the self-destruction and atrocities before most. Some of my fellow officers, by their offhand comments and guarded looks, began to realize the war was not going to turn out well. I couldn't be sure whom I could trust. It was difficult."

Herr Mueller continued, "The day finally came I removed the Nazi pin from my uniform. I needed someone to trust, if only for my own sanity. It was heavily on my mind as I strolled the art galleries in Florence. I saw a priest roaming the gallery, examining exhibits, taking notes. I was not a religious man, so I felt uneasy approaching him. He must have sensed it. An hour later, in another room, we spoke for the first time.

"As summer days went by, occasionally, I saw him at various galleries. Always, interesting conversation resulted. At first, we talked about art, then philosophy, science but never about the war. I think he knew I was conflicted.

"Eventually, I felt I could trust him with my deepest secret. One day, I said to Father Lombardi there was something that I had told to no one.

"'Was it something you can tell me?'

"I told him it was about the war and how I could wear the uniform but could no longer support the Nazi cause.

"'That would be dangerous for you, Frederick.'

"You don't know how dangerous. I could be sent to the Russian front! But still, I don't know.

"'Why are you conflicted?' he asked.

"I lamented, 'There is so much evil in the world. Atrocities are being committed, but we are afraid to mention them. Yet we are to be a super race.'

"Father Lombardi said, 'How can you have a super race with no soul, with no compassion for your fellow man? You cannot change the world without the spirit. Your small act of defiance has set you on a path to self-atonement.'

"That small act could get me sent to the Russian front or worse.

"'And I would not want to see that my friend, but removing that Nazi pin from your coat means so much more than that! You cannot give in to evil once you are committed to the good.'

"But why does your God not stop it?

"Father Lombardi said, 'That is something Christians often ask when confronted with tragedy.'

"Lombardi told a story about a friend who was taking care of his newborn baby. The friend was changing the baby on a high table. As he turned away just to grab a diaper, the baby rolled over off the table and, unfortunately, died. The man abandoned his faith because he believed God had killed his baby. Lombardi tried to console his friend by explaining that God may allow tragedy, but He does not will it."

"And what did you say to Father Lombardi?"

"I said he had faith in the good over evil. I had not."

"Herr Mueller, it amazes me that after all these years, you can remember so clearly. You were both young. I don't know what it was like during the war."

"I remember those years as clearly as if it had happened yesterday. Father Lombardi was young, only twenty-eight when he was killed."

"That is a tragedy," I said.

Herr Mueller replied, "But I think he knew it, I mean what was going to happen to him."

"How so? How could he have known?"

"Intuition? An angel spoke to him? I don't know. He asked me what I would do after the war. I told him of an art gallery somewhere in Heidelberg and would look forward to him coming to see it. He told me he would have liked that very much, but he had something he had to do." Herr Mueller sighed. "God allows tragedy. He does not will it."

My host emptied his glass, perhaps to deaden his sorrowful memories. Looking more optimistic, he put it down. "Saturday morning starts early in my gallery." Standing away from the table he said, "If you get cold tonight, there are extra blankets in the closet. I will see you before you go. Sleep well, my friend."

So that was it. I had all the information there was. Morning would bring an early start back to Rome. There was only one chance to redeem the church. Mueller knew no one would believe an ex-Nazi. The famous canvas would have to be discovered.

I uttered a quick prayer about the Fiat, that it would cross the Alps again on icy roads. A longer prayer concerned stopping at the abbey and the dreaded return of the memoirs of Saint Benedict to Monsignor Romano's private collection. I was sure to receive a harsh rebuke for taking it.

But overall, there was a sense that a corner had been turned. I remembered the people I'd met along the way. I'd have time to think about them on the highway. This curious traveler had learned more than he could have ever imagined, seen so much more than he'd have seen on a farm in Maine.

Predawn Saturday, I was awakened by Herr Mueller shuffling around the kitchen. There was nothing now to hold me back from getting on the road over the Alps. I threw back the warm blankets, and my warm feet touched a cold floor. I went to the window as the first golden sunlight blushed the high castle spires across the foggy river. I took it as a positive sign.

By the time I bounded downstairs, Mueller had raised the blinds. He had unboxed more clay figures and swept the gallery for the weekend. The faint sigh of the stove warmed our "Guten morgens." He handed me a cup of steaming coffee. "Thank you, Herr Mueller." I paused. "You have helped in ways I never expected."

"Before you go, please, wait." He walked to the back of the shop to an antique desk cluttered with boxes. He took out a small key from his vest pocket and unlocked the top drawer. He hesitated for only a moment as he held on to a small black book. Mueller turned to me and said, "I have something you should have. His church should have it." He thrust it into my hands, as if not wanting to let it go, but it was the right thing to do. "These are his words, the diary of Father Lombardi! He secretly slipped it into my coat pocket in the back seat of the gestapo staff car. I have read it many times. You may see something that will help enlighten the people of Sant' Ambrogio."

I was overwhelmed by his gesture.

Herr Mueller added, "You know, you remind me of him. He had as many questions as you do. And like you, he fought for his church."

"Because of you," I replied, "people will know the real truth about Father Lombardi and the man who helped him."

The bell over the door tinkled as I opened it. He said one more thing. "You will let me know regardless of what happens?"

"Yes, Herr Mueller, I will, whatever happens. *Auf Wiedersehen.*"

We warmly clinched hands. I went on my way.

The Fiat's little engine was cold, so it took a few cranks to start. While it warmed up, a hymn I'd first heard as a child in church came to me: "Go out into the darkness and put your hand into the hand of God. That shall be better than light and safer than a known way."

*****

The road wound with the river to the outskirts of town. I wanted to drive straight through to Florence, bursting with the good news. No tourist trip this time, no excursions up scenic mountain roads. There would be only one stop about seven hours ahead: the abbey of Saint Benedict. I would be there by early afternoon. The quiet solitude of the abbey would give me a chance to pore over Lombardi's diary for any clue as to where he might have hidden the painting. Beneath all my thoughts was the undeniable desire to see Frances George.

I stopped at a petrol station on the edge of the city. Gunther, a good-natured fellow, checked the oil, petrol, and tires. He asked where I was going. When I told him, he said, "I think today it should be calm in the mountains."

I took the autobahn, then turned off on the old pilgrim road into Switzerland. Lakes, vales, and villages sidled by with barely a notice. I was deep in thoughtful anticipation of whatever might happen.

After crossing the Swiss border on a clear upward plain, the Fiat popped a tire. I'd changed tires before; it should have been easy. After looking under the hood, in the rear engine compartment and, although unlikely, under the car, I found the jack beneath the driver's seat. Everything would be fine now, just a short inconvenience. But the lug nuts were hard to loosen, and the jack sank into the frozen mud on the side of the road. I bloodied my knuckles in the process.

After changing the tire, I threw the tools on the rear floorboard. I remained for a while to enjoy white clouds reflected on an emerald lake, rainbows and waterfalls shimmering in the sun.

Up the grade to higher elevations, the road was clear. Down the way I'd come, there hadn't been a car in miles. The faint sound of music broke the silence. It rumbled up the mountain road. The blue and white Chevy van filled with Americans having the time of their lives worked its way up the mountain. A light cloud of dust trailed behind it. They waved and called out "Hi, hello," as they swished right by. I'm sure they did not know that I, too, was an American. But no matter, to get to my destination by late afternoon, there'd be no time to linger.

The little Fiat ran like a top the rest of the day. I entered the gates of the abbey no later than three in the afternoon. It was just when the kids had been let out of school. Some of them saw me drive up the hill and ran to the car, shouting, "Father Conley! Father Conley is back!"

Alex, the born leader, the beautiful Geena, tough little Luca, and the inseparable sisters Emilia and Sofia ran to me, laughing, clutching onto my robe, and, of course, began to ask a lot of questions. Alex said, "I knew you would come back."

Luca shot back, "I was the one who said it first."

"So you were both right," I said.

Geena spoke for the others. "Father Conley, will you stay with us so you can be our teacher?"

"What about Sister Hensel?" I asked.

Her cute little face flustered. "Well, I guess we already have a nice teacher."

Luca said, "Yes, one that puts me in the corner all the time!"

Emilia piped up, "For pulling our hair!"

Sofia scorned Luca. "We like Sister Hensel. Very much, we do."

Up the hill, I heard a familiar bright voice, calling, "John! I see you've come back."

From the schoolhouse door, a smiling Frances George hailed my arrival. She strode down the grade to where I was surrounded by the children. "Go along, kids. I will see you at school in the morning."

"Say goodbye to Father Conley," said Alex.

Luca rolled his eyes. "Goodbye...uh, John. Last one down the hill is a smelly porcupine!"

They ran, tagging their way down to the road. By the time they were out of sight and sound, Frances was standing close to me. I said, "It's nice to see you, Frances. I was hoping I would."

Her concerned eyes foreshadowed her query, "The *Saint Mary*, did you find it?"

"Not exactly. Well, I know it is not in Germany. But listen to this! I was given a diary that might tell us what Father Lombardi was up against on the night he disappeared.

"Up against?"

"I was told Farther Lombardi was not the man I thought he was. I am sorry for that. We could have read his pages here at the abbey, but I don't know if I'll be staying tonight."

"But you just got here. What would be a reason for your going so soon?"

"I have to return Saint Benedict's memoir. To put it mildly, the monsignor must be annoyed that I carelessly took it from has library."

With a laugh, she said, "You're so lucky, my friend. Monsignor Romano is in Spain, not expected to return for several days."

"Jeez! I've been dreading his rebuke ever since I felt the book in the bottom of my rucksack. Anyway, I pray may God be with him on his long journey."

"Well, then, since you will be staying after all, I will meet you in the meditation room at the top of the stairs at sunset."

We embraced as if we were old friends.

With a deep breath of fresh, cool mountain air, I climbed the granite stairs into the foyer and straight to Monsignor's library. I turned the bronze handle and peered in. It was empty; the coast was clear. Quickly, I went in, found the place behind the glass where the book of Saint Benedict belonged, and slipped it back into its place. Gregorian chant echoed from the great hall. I had not been seen going in or coming out. I felt like a child who thought he'd gotten away with something but knew he really hadn't.

The Diary of Father Lombardi

It was a cozy study warmed by a blazing fire, with arched windows laden with heavily embroidered drapes on either side of the hearth. There was a red handwoven carpet covering a planked oak floor and wonderfully comfortable cabin-style chairs and colorful craftsman lamps.

Peering through the window, I saw the slow drift of snow building on the boughs of the evergreens. The sky was darkened by heavy gray clouds over a faint amber glow where the sun had just sunk below the horizon. I opened the diary and leafed through its elegant pages. Its phrases were poetically penned. It was dated January 1, 1944, through August 3, the last day the unfortunate priest had been seen alive in Florence.

I was just beginning to read when a flustered Frances George entered the room, smiling and carrying a curious basket. While she unpacked it, she said, "Oh, I've been rushing all day! Couldn't wait to read with you! I've brought cheese and bread and sweet grapes from Sicily in case we get hungry. Have you started examining the diary?"

I said, "Not really, just leafed through the pages. It seems Father Lombardi was a highly educated but solitary priest. So far, I've learned that he was probably more comfortable in his books, in the study of the arts, than with the people of his congregation."

I put another log on the fire and stoked it with the iron poker, causing red cinders to swirl. Frances speculated. "That may have been a reason he was so misunderstood."

Evening bells chimed at twilight, and the chant rose from the monks' chapel. We moved our chairs together in front of the hearth and browsed through the leather-bound pages. A cover page referenced prayers he had prayed for blessing the new year.

1 January 1944

I have prayed continually for an end to this war. So many have suffered, so many have need-lessly died. They say it may be over by the end of the year, but I know little of these things. So I pray and lead my church in prayer. I have recently been assigned to the small church of St. Ambrogio in Florence. It is a fine and pros-perous church of long traditions. On Sundays its pews are filled with faithful parishioners. I pray, Oh God, that I can lead them through these sorrowful days.

16 April 1944

It was a pleasant spring day. Cool air carried the fragrant scent of wisteria. A wedding filled our church with flowers, and dreams and aspi-rations were seen on the faces of the newly-weds. The groom was dressed in high-cuffed pants and an oversized collar. There was no explanation for it! Although, it added to the carnival atmosphere. The bride wore a simple white dress. After the vows, the wedding party marched down Via Dei Macci with drums and horns. Children waved ribbons and old women gossiped, strolling behind the wedding parade. Old men watched from benches along the way and drank their red wine. There, no one seemed concerned with their hardships.

1 May 1944

While browsing the halls of the Uffizi Gallery, I met a Capt. Mueller from the German consulate. His knowledge of the arts is impressive. He seems highly educated and cordial. For a Wehrmacht officer, I sensed something extraordinarily human about him. At times I feel, as the mystery reveals itself, my story has already been written.

14 May 1944

On Sunday, the sky was wet. The mood in the town, gloomy. A renown and beloved duchess committed suicide last night by jumping from a tower. Her body was found near the river Arno at dawn. The war has turned many toward the church. Some pray desperately, sadly. I realized there are more hearts broken in the world than can be mended.

I fashioned my sermon on the subject of kindness.

"So many are having doubts. But God has
    given you a way to know
that He has not deserted you. You will see Him
    in your own kindness,

your understanding and your generosity. You
    will know Him in every
sunset that is followed by another sunrise..."

Signore Corsi, of the market association, said
that he liked the sermon, asked for a blessing,
and also reminded me that the war was bad for
business.

6 June 1944
Today is a day to rejoice! Rome has been liberated! And in the afternoon, we learned that
the Allies have landed in Normandy. There is
a cautious excitement in the air. For the people
know the war is not yet over, and the Fascists are
still watching.

25 July 1944
This morning, bells rang at the great cathedral as
I rang the modest bell of St. Ambrogio. Benito
Mussolini has been removed from power! King
Emanuel said the war is lost. It was pleasant
and warm with celebrations in the piazzas and
laughter in the streets. Father Bruno and I will
begin to prepare for a very special Festival of
Sant' Maria in the fall.

28 July 1944
This afternoon, Capt. Mueller bought coffee at
Cafe Salvini on the banks of the Arno River. He
was open about his doubts of the Nazi cause.
His Nazi insignia was no longer pinned to his

lapel. I will not write more about what was said in case of my diary falls into unfriendly hands, with the exception that we both understood the gravity of the situation. And it has confirmed to me that Capt. Muller is a man of conscience. An hour ago, a man cautiously entered the back door of the sanctuary, where I was sweeping. Much troubled, He had come to see a priest. I led him into the privacy of the confessional. We prayed together through the black curtain. He confessed he had killed a German soldier and he was at that moment being pursued by the Gestapo. He said he was with the Resistance. We prayed that God forgive his sins. As I stepped out of the booth, he was already disappearing into the darkness.

1 August 1944

Late last night, the telephone rang in the rectory. Capt. Mueller was on the other end of the line. He said the and the army would be moving north in a few days and he was questioned by Gestapo Colonel Ziegler about artworks in the church of St. Ambrogio. He warned the Nazi Colonel will take whatever they can as he rounds up the resistance. Ziegler believes that I have been aiding its leaders. Mueller begged me to leave the city, go to the Vatican for my own safety. But I will stay with my church to help in whatever way I can.

3 August 1944

A dawn, there was much activity by the Germans. Trucks moving, troops going north. With tanks and guns, the whole army is evacuating.

Soon, the air was shocked by the crackle of gun shots. Not, single shots, but several shots all at once. In only a few minutes, Signore Corsi burst in, sweaty, agitated, reporting that the partisans are being executed. I know my life is in grave danger from the underground, who believe I have collaborated with the Nazis. After much prayer, I've decided to send Father Bruno to the Vatican over his protests. He will carry a letter to our bishop that may explain why he cannot be here tonight and how St. Ambrogio may continue its traditions after the war. The day worsens as the massacre of civilians continues. A notice was nailed on the church door just as they were posted in the streets. The patrols of the German armed forces have been ordered to shoot at anyone who is found on the street or who appears at the windows. I was told they are mining the bridges that cross the Arno. Soldiers aggressively marched citizens off the streets, out of the piazzas. A dark cloud has descended onto our city. I am alone, sequestered in this sanctuary. It is only a matter of hours.

*****

Before dawn, the morning dove declared the start of a mild day. Frances and I sat there in silence for a moment, no longer attached to the earth, staring at dying embers. Father Lombardi's story had come to an end. I realized we were sitting close, closer than when we began. Frances lifted her head from my shoulder and turned to look into my eyes.

Tears ran down her saddened face. She reached for my hand, and mine did not slip away. She was angry. "His friend tried to warn him! In all the places I've traveled, of all the people I have known, sometimes a priest is hardest for me to understand. He died for a simple painting! The galleries are filled with paintings. Why did he sacrifice his life? He could have taken Mueller's advice. He could have gone with Father Bruno to the Vatican."

I tried to give his perspective. "Father Lombardi advised Herr Mueller, you cannot give in to evil once you have committed to the good. He couldn't have known he would have to give up his life. He was a priest dedicated to the church, not unlike other men who face life or death. There's a price to pay for willing dedication that few are ready to pay. In the end, he did not die for an icon. He died for devotion, for the people of his parish."

Return to Rome

After a long, insightful night exploring Father Lombardi's last faithful account, we were spent. Stretching and yawning, Frances noticed by her watch that her shift at the clinic would start at six. Just time enough to grab a cup of coffee. I'd try to get some rest before heading back to Rome.

I drew the chamber curtains close against the rising sun and lay there for only an hour. The excitement of getting back to the Vatican with the diary overcame my need for sleep. *No time to shave the stubble off my face. Just pack the bag and get going.*

Frances was surely on her clinic rounds. Of course, the suggestion that we have a life together was unfeasible. She was as dedicated to the help of the sick as I was to help those in need of faith. I did not see her before I left. Yet even then, I believed she would always be part of my life.

An amiable monk in the kitchen prepared something to eat for my journey. The Fiat coasted down the drive then turned south via the old Pilgrim Highway. Uplifted and emboldened, the main thing was to get my thoughts together for the report to Monsignor DeLuca.

Even the old Fiat seemed to have new strength, powering its way up the steep grades and gliding down the other sides. The sun rose as lakes and forests whooshed by. By ten o'clock, the Italian plain came into view. Tuscany was now only an hour away, Vatican City a few more.

The first thing I thought was how I would explain my own account, to create a record of my discovery. The account of Father Lombardi would mean so much to so many. Thoughts kept running through a sleepless mind that had immensely increased in its belief in divine intervention. It began in Andermatt and Greta's suggestion I meet Friar Gelder, whom she knew only by his reputation as a "wise man." He led me to Pastor Braun and through the back alleys of East Berlin. Then seemingly out of nowhere, Herr Mueller provided the diary.

The whole journey seemed to add up. I see now that what I thought were dead ends were all part of a prewritten chronicle. And I no longer believed Granacci's painting had been taken by Colonel Ziegler. Friar Gelder, Pastor Braun, and Herr Mueller were no bureaucrats. They had recovered stolen art, searched for meaning in ancient cultures, helped hundreds of Jews to escape the death camps, and tracked down Nazi leaders. Dr. Frances George left the luxury of wealth to volunteer in medical clinics and remote refugee camps. Any young priest would truly be blessed to have such mentors.

*****

By 2:00 a.m., the dependable Fiat was parked at the Vatican. I walked through its phenomenal halls to Monsignor DeLuca's open chamber door. He was consumed in paperwork neatly stacked on his desk. I lightly knocked. Monsignor DeLuca looked up, smiled, and placed his eyeglasses on the desk. He stood up with both arms outstretched and greeted me as a prodigal son. "Father Conley, we have been awaiting your return! It seems a long two weeks since we last saw you."

"It seems much longer to me," I said.

He led me to a chair, saying, "Come, sit here while I make tea."

Father Moretti appeared at the door. "Father Conley, what a wonderful surprise! We have prayed that you would have a safe and pleasant journey."

"Undoubtedly, that is how I am here today."

DeLuca said, "You will please tell us everything."

Moretti chimed in, "Yes, we were hoping for some exciting news."

"I have much to tell. My journey was both perilous and enlightening."

Moretti asked, "Did you ever find this, what was his name… Captain—"

DeLuca reminded him, "Captain Mueller."

"Before I tell you about Mueller, I have something to show you." I brought out the leather-covered diary and handed it to Monsignor DeLuca as Mueller had handed it to me. Monsignor DeLuca asked, "And what is this?"

"This diary of a dedicated priest are the accounts of Father Lombardi."

"Amazing!" responded Father Moretti.

Monsignor DeLuca replied, "Yes, astounding! Wherever did you find it?"

"It was given to me by a confidant of Father Lombardi. He once wrote this man was a man of conscience. I was given the diary by a man who has traveled the world, seeking knowledge— Frederick Mueller."

Father DeLuca commented, "When seeking continues, the possibility of knowing exists."

I said, "I assure you, concerning Frederick Mueller, that is the case."

The book was opened, and the priests commented on various notations. They soon noticed that I was fading for lack of sleep. A nun was called to lead me to my chamber, while DeLuca and Moretti contemplated the written accounts of Father Lombardi.

My first night at the Vatican was peaceful and comforting. I awoke before dawn. My eyes cleared, staring at frescoed angels. My head still swimming from the days before, morning prayers were whispered as I knelt at my bedside. In a painted chapel, my prayers for a resolution of my mission persisted. After I savored a brisk breakfast of sweet pastry and hot cappuccino at the lobby café, I prepared for what the day might bring.

I returned to Monsignor DeLuca's office at six. It appeared that they had been poring over the diary all night, no longer skeptical of rumors repeated for the past four decades. They now realized, as I had, what a great injustice had been done. The ramifications of this new revelation would go far beyond Florence. Monsignor DeLuca grasped my hand, saying, "Do you realize what you have accomplished? You may have saved the reputation of the church more than you realize. We all knew during the war questionable actions were taken by some in the church, including cooperation with the Nazi government. To this day, these contradictions have left a scar on the church, perhaps a memory that will not be forgotten." He sighed. "Now we pray that Father Lombardi will not be forgotten either. His diary has shone a new light on the church, one that will shine forever on the true meaning of dedication to the Holy See."

I reflected for a moment on a poem: "During your times of trial and suffering, when you see only one set of footprints, it was then that I carried you." He had guided this humble servant across the frozen mountains and through dark nights.

Father Moretti said, "We can help you now, Father Conley."

Monsignor DeLuca made current their speculations. "On that last fateful day, the diary mentions a letter containing a message to Bishop Scozza. We've already discovered His Eminence was not at the Vatican to receive it. In fact, his whereabouts were unknown."

I remembered, "Yes, I'd asked Father Bruno if he knew what was in the envelope. He told me he had not opened it. He only delivered it to the bishop's office."

"Is it possible the bishop did not see Lombardi's letter?" Asked Monsignor DeLuca.

Moretti added, "Father Lombardi's diary notes that the letter would explain how the church would continue its traditions in the future."

DeLuca said, "A thorough search into the archives has been requested."

I again found myself in the subfloors of the Vatican among its vast catalogs, searching for a lonely envelope addressed to a bishop who passed ten years earlier. Hours had flown by when a young intern came with an old folder. It was labeled, "SAINT AMBROGIO—Florence, Italy."

The young lady said, "The folder had not been filed where it should have been under the "Church of Sant'Ambrogio." It had been misfiled under Saint Ambrogio, the bishop of Milan, who had built many churches."

I discovered a tattered old parchment and an unopened envelope, brown with age. The folder was lain out on a heavy oak desk, where I contemplated the envelope, sealed by a determined priest in a desperate hour. The fact that it had not been opened had perhaps answered a deeper question, the lasting disgrace on the church. Father Lombardi had sent it in order to, in his words, usher in the future traditions of Sant' Ambrogio. Instead, those traditions had been forgotten.

I reached down into the Levi's I wore under my robes for my old pocketknife and, using the small blade, cut open the envelope. As I looked inside, I realized it contained one slip of paper, folded in half. Father Lombardi had not written a long explanation, a plea, or even a prayer. There was only one phrase in his own hand: "Quo est Verum," written in a language which I was not fluent. If in 1978 we'd had smartphones, the meaning could have been easily searched. As it was, the young intern brought to the desk a Latin-English dictionary, a resource always available in the archives.

Quo est was simple enough. It meant "this is." *Verum* was it, this is verified, or this is real? I flipped the pages to find a translation. It read, "This is true." But what was true? How vague it sounded. Was it some kind of riddle, a code only Bishop Scozza would understand? Unfortunately, the answer to the riddle had probably been lost forever. Again, a frustrating dead end.

There was another old piece of parchment in the folder. I carefully unfolded its brittle pages onto the desk. The left side first, then the right, then I slowly opened one more fold from top to bottom. The charcoal ink was faded. My eyes adjusted to a sketch of a church foundation. At the bottom was written, "Ambrogio's Church."

Fascinating, but nothing special, until I noticed a sketch within the walls. There was a rough drawing of a stairway and some kind of chamber underfoot. A short notation was scribbled beneath it. The writing was small, stained, and faded. In the top desk drawer was a magnifying glass. The interpretation was, "Where the saints sleep." A tomb or catacomb under the church?

With the cryptic message on a water-stained parchment, I jumped up flights of marble stairs. Through seemingly endless halls, I jogged all the way back to Monsignor DeLuca's chamber. Before opening the door, I paused for a moment to compose myself. We would all know the one thing left was to locate the entrance to the hidden catacombs. "Monsignor DeLuca, I believe we have found the golden key."

He questioned, "The golden key?"

He began to examine the parchment I laid in front of him, murmuring something about Father Lombardi. He wondered aloud, "How could he have known these forgotten secrets?"

I calmly recollected, "Father Bruno has been at the church, worked at the church for most of his life. He must know every square inch of it by now. I also have swept the floors and cleaned the statues. Neither one of us have ever seen any clue there was a concealed chamber."

Father Moretti came in almost unnoticed. "But it must be there! It's the only explanation where a painting of that size could have been hidden."

I suddenly realized, "Unless...unless...Father Lombardi had himself placed the parchment in the folder."

Moretti added, "Yes, he was a scholar. He must have been more than familiar with the Ambrogio files."

Monsignor DeLuca stood up and evaluated the situation. "It is clear now what steps must be taken."

I was surprised at what he said next. "His Holiness will want to be updated. He has been aware of this mission and has asked us to keep him informed of any progress."

DeLuca picked up the phone and dialed three numbers. By his respectful, somber tone, I realized he had been transferred to Pope John Paul. "Yes, Your Holiness, we have found documents of interest that may lead us to a fruitful conclusion. Yes, Your Holiness. No, Your Holiness. Do I have your permission to excavate if necessary? As always, I will keep you informed. *Grazie.* God be with you."

Quid est Verum

On Tuesday of the next week, Sant' Ambrogio was abuzz with activity and anticipation. Italian security forces already surrounded the block as workmen set up construction lights and covered the delicate marble floors with heavy tarps. The parchment's crude drawing of Sant' Ambrogio's foundation was not specific as to the location of the vault, nor was there any indication of an entrance.

Vatican archaeologists systematically sonar-scanned the area around Granacci's tomb, hoping to locate any empty space behind the walls or under the floor. The possibility of discovering the lost truth grew more palpable by the minute. An order of nuns gathered at the altar where they prayed for a revelation.

In the alcove, after fifty years of failing his disgraced church, Father Bruno experienced his own regressive meltdown. Hearing of Father Lombardi's diary, he reacted with well-practiced doubt. Even after I'd told him Mueller's story, he had only nodded with concern. With all the activity in the sanctuary, Father Bruno resumed taking bronze and silver accoutrements to be secured in a safer place.

Herr Mueller arrived from Heidelberg on the deutsche train. A sliver of sunlight appeared at the southern door as he stepped in, not far from where Father Bruno was working. I wondered if they'd actually met in those long days past. In a previous life, Captain Mueller had visited Father Lombardi at the church once or twice. My suspicions were confirmed as, despite the decades that had passed between them, they seemed to recognize each other. I concealed myself behind a granite column in order to eavesdrop.

The old priest cautiously approached Herr Mueller. Their lives were a world apart. Father Bruno seemed twenty years his elder. In disbelief, he greeted the former German captain with a pleasant smile, an expression I had not seen on his face in the entire time I'd known him. He reached out a welcoming hand to the taller figure obscured by the light beaming in behind him. "You are Frederick Mueller! I was told by the young priest that you have been of tremendous help."

Mueller pulled the old door shut behind him. "Brother Bruno, can you forgive me?"

Father Bruno said, "But why? You have nothing to be forgiven for. It is I…it is the congregation that has mischaracterized you, blamed you for their faithless catastrophe."

Mueller responded, "I could have come—should have come—years ago. I only thought Father Lombardi's goodness would have been discovered days after it had been lost. There would have been no need to return to a place that would only remind me of sorrow. It's true I did not know of your troubles. If I had, believe me, you would have seen me without delay!"

Father Bruno said, "All of us need forgiveness, my friend. Yet we, in some way, are responsible for those who have allowed superstition and rumor to shut our eyes."

My own joyful eyes damped as the two new compatriots embraced. I retreated to the open air and pondered in the sunlight. I watched *polizia* who were posted around the church.

When not more than five minutes had passed, a green-and-red cab pulled up. I glimpsed someone pay the fee before the door opened. Frances stepped out. She gave instructions to the driver, handing him a few more lira. "*Per favore*, take my bags to Hotel Bernini." She looked up smiling. "John!"

By now, we had grown to the point that I allowed her to call me by my Christian name, except in the company of other clergy.

Surprised to see her there, I exclaimed, "Dr. George, it's nice to see you."

"Miss me?"

I felt awkward and a little embarrassed. "Well, you know… yes. What a great surprise. I just didn't expect to see you at Sant' Ambrogio!"

Coyly, she inquired, "Did you really think I could be kept away?"

At Saint Benedict's, we read the diary in front of a warm hearth in secluded intimacy. At Sant'Ambrogio, we'd have to avoid any inappropriate appearances. Reassuringly, she said, "As far as anyone knows, I've come because I read the diary."

"Then let's go in," I said. "I'd like to introduce you to some very interesting people."

We walked through the bronze doors to the gathering of the priests and Herr Mueller. Workmen were setting up lights, and others were laying canvas down to protect the marble floors. Several hours of scrutinizing cracks in the rock floors for any sign of an elusive chamber, one of the archaeologists noted that the floor was made of large pieces of marble weighing several hundred pounds apiece.

Fathers DeLuca and Moretti had been sent by His Holiness to observe and report the progress of the search. Monsignor DeLuca's question arose, "How could Father Lombardi alone have lifted the stones?"

An archaeologist replied, "Moreover, there was no evidence of tampering or even a gap between the well-fitted marble sections. Therefore, how could the heavy blocks be moved without leaving a single scratch?"

There was someone else I was hoping to see, and like an apparition, she appeared in the second-row pew, praying. She lifted her veil as I knelt near her. I made room for Frances. "Signora Campinella, I'd like to introduce you to someone. This is Frances. She is also an American."

The old Italian woman looked her over skeptically. "She is not Italian?"

"I am surprised at you, Rosalie!"

"Do you believe in the goodness of the saints, young lady?"

"Dr. George is a volunteer at Saint Benedict in the Alps," I said.

"And you are Catholic?"

Although I knew Frances was Protestant, she diplomatically offered, "I believe Sant' Ambrogio to be the house of God, Signora Campinella."

Rosalie's face beamed her blessing. "My grandparents and generations before, God rest their souls, prayed in this sanctuary. Now if you believe in its resurrection, you are also a daughter of my church."

*****

Floors and walls had been scrutinized with the most advanced sonar. Frances and I conversed with the experts while they inspected the building from corner to corner. Statues had been moved and replaced. At a certain point, workmen who had come at dawn began rolling up the tarps. The search in the sanctuary was not going well. We were running out of places to look.

We were standing near the altar when Monsignor DeLuca and Moretti walked across the marble floor and spoke to us. Monsignor DeLuca glanced at Moretti and said, "I am sorry, Father Conley, but it is getting late, and we are expected at the

Vatican. There is no shame in hope, but now, it is almost certain that Father Bruno will be retired, and this church will be annexed by the great cathedral."

Father Moretti chimed in, "But for you, there are special plans. You have shown your dedication is true. There is something we'd like to talk to you about. Would you come see us next week?"

I assured them that I would. They turned away and walked out the door behind the nuns who had been praying with Rosalie Campanella for the resurrection of the church.

Frances and I stood there as optimists with an empty feeling. It was then she noticed the etched scriptures on the front of the altar. She interpreted one aloud. "Lean not on your own understanding, and he will show you the way."

I was familiar with one carved along the east wall. "Call unto me and I shall answer you and show you great and mighty things that you do not know."

We followed the scriptures around the sanctuary. "And let us not grow weary while doing good, for in due season, we shall reap a harvest if we do not lose heart," was engraved under a marble bust of Saint Francis of Assisi.

On the pedestal elevating the figure of Saint Ambrogio, it read, "God is not accustomed to refusing a good gift to those who ask for one."

We made our way to the marble tomb in the alcove. Once again, we read the name on the bronze plaque, Francesco Granacci. Wistfully, I said, "Here lies the Renaissance artist who painted our elusive *Santa Maria*."

The tomb set upon two granite steps on a dais. Rectangular in shape, it was about four feet high, six feet long, two and a half feet wide. Its simple design looked like a framed stone box. The headstone was milled out of a marble slab five inches thick. Below the bronze plaque was engraved a palm wreath. On the edge of the headstone was a simple Latin phrase. I told Frances, "I've read this before. It means 'God's gifts lift the world.'"

She read it again. "God's gifts lift the world."

"An appropriate statement, isn't it, for an artist of such great talent?" I said.

"You know, John, we all have a gift or two. You have your gift for seeking out truth."

I returned the compliment. "And you have the gift of comforting and healing the poor. If everyone would just discover their gift and work for it, the world would be lifted."

As I said it, she leaned in more closely to inspect the engraving on the stone. "Wait…John, look here! This is not a full sentence. At the end, there's a comma!"

I also looked closely then felt it to make sure. "It is a comma. I hadn't noticed that before. Where's the rest of the sentence?"

Stepping up on the platform, we followed the script around the corner to the side of the stone. She saw it first. "Here it says, 'Quia ille solus novit.'"

I translated, "'For He only knows.' For He only knows what? That's all very interesting but—"

She said, "But there's another comma!"

We peered around the back where there was a space between the tomb and the wall. It was only about thirty inches wide. We were dumbfounded when we read the script. I said, "I can't believe it! 'Quid est verum!' It's the message from Father Lombardi!"

"Yes," she said. "The whole thing reads, 'God's gifts lift the world, for He only knows what is true.' We found it!"

"No," I realized. "We didn't find it. We were led to it."

There was something different below the words. Nowhere else on the tomb was a protruding marble pediment. I put my hands on the stone and pushed to the left, but it wouldn't budge. "Well," I said, "It couldn't have been that easy."

Frances gently moved me aside. "Here, let me try." When she pushed it to the right, we heard a click. Behind the tomb, the floor moved, maybe an inch. I put my foot on the marble and pushed down, and the whole granite slab began to swivel. By pushing a little harder, it opened wider, causing cool, musty air to rise from deep below. We peered into the darkness below and heard the silence of a thousand years.

As I peered into the tight space, my hands began to sweat. My anxiety notched up with the thought of going down the exposed narrow stairway. Frances stood up, turned around, and called out into the sanctuary, "It's here!" She ran to the main door, where priests and workmen had gathered to say their goodbyes. She excitingly shouted, "Monsignor DeLuca, we've found the concealed chamber!"

For a second, a hundred surprised faces in the piazza stared without making a sound. Then as if a light had been switched on, the entire gaggle of onlookers erupted in a cheer. They ran back into the basilica. The police quickly formed a line in order to halt the crowd of newspaper and TV reporters from rushing in. Suddenly the sanctuary was again filled with excitement and loud speculation.

In spite of my fear of narrow spaces, I borrowed a flashlight from a workman whose job it was to go down below the floor. Frances sensed my apprehension. "You don't have to go down there, you know. It's the workman's job."

As I peered down into the hole on my hands and knees, Herr Mueller said, "It is you who must finish the journey, Father Conley."

A light beam cut through the darkness, down several steps to the dusty floor. There was only one thing to do. I was compelled by my greater spirit to climb into the hole and down the tight passageway. With no railing on the stairway and nothing to catch my balance, I carefully took the first step, then the next, lowering myself slowly, cautiously.

As the light flashed ahead into the cold chamber, the darkness enveloped me. A thin, lanky archaeologist by the name of Lorenzo, strapped on his tool belt and came down the steps right behind me. "You may need my help, father."

Our light beams crossed on the walls aged with faded Tuscan paint. Lorenzo exclaimed, "This catacomb is much older than we imagined!"

We saw a Christian fish carved on the arch above the passageway. I looked up to the faces waiting in anticipation for some word. I signaled, "Nothing yet."

We pressed through a narrow limestone entry into an early Christian burial chamber. I reflected, "These graves were concealed from Roman desecration."

Lorenzo pointed out footprints in the dust. "Though someone has walked this floor more recently."

What digger would not want to explore this cavern? But for now, we were looking for one thing and one thing only. We turned to retrace our steps back to the stairway, anxious faces still waiting for a sign. My light made a thorough search around the walls crowded with the dead. An unmistakable feeling came over me that an end of my search was very near.

As I turned around, the beam caught a glimpse of something wedged behind the rock stairway. "Lorenzo, please, could you hold the flashlight?" It would require both hands to pull the canvas-covered object out of its hiding place.

Lorenzo handed me a cloth I used to wipe off fifty years of dust. Under the canvas, to keep it dry, the frame was wrapped in waxed paper and tightly tied with brown twine. It was heavy enough that we wondered how Father Lombardi, by himself, carried it to its hiding place, for it was not easy for both of us to hand it up the stairs and awaiting anxious arms. Mueller and Father Bruno carried it to a table and placed it under the remaining work lamp.

We all gathered around its concealed frame of approximately four by five feet. Father Bruno commented, "It is the right size for the Virgin painting."

I cut the string with my pocketknife and unfolded the covering, much like I had unfolded the parchment blueprint in the Vatican archives. When we saw it, there were jubilant shouts of, "Bravo," within the walls of the old sanctuary and tears in the eyes of Father Bruno. There she was, saints gathered around her, embracing her holy child in the beautiful, colorful oil. Murmurs and gasps attested to its perfection. All knew something profound had changed.

A moment later, reporters and cameramen broke through the police line. They surrounded the painting and instantly began shouting questions. Flashbulbs exploded by the dozens. A media firestorm started. In a matter of hours, the news carried the truth about Father Lombardi, and so the redemption of Sant' Ambrogio astonished the world.

The Vigil

Journalists rushed off to file their reports in time for the evening news. Someone told us that Rome Reports had announced that there would be a vigil at Piazza Ambrogio and a celebration for the hero that should be named a saint, Father Lombardi.

Herr Mueller came to me with an open smile. We grasped each other's arms as brothers. I told him, "There's a vigil tonight in front of the church. Will I see you there?"

"No, but thank you. I can't stay. I have seen a good man, my great friend, back in his people's hearts." I saw passion in his eyes when he said, "I will forever be grateful for that. But this is not a place for this old German solder. It's my karma. You, my friend, have an interest in the arts, I know. When you again find your thirst for adventure, I can show you the world! As for now, I will travel by train back to Heidelberg."

"Then what will you do next, Herr Mueller?"

"A clay Minoan goddess waits for me on the island of Crete!" He confidently shook my hand and stole out a side door on his way to places yet unknown.

At dusk, the people of Florence began to arrive, carrying flowers and glowing candles. They placed them on the granite steps and around the church doors. I couldn't help remembering what was written in Lombardi's diary. These were the same doors where the gestapo had nailed their "threat of death" curfew. Now these were doors open to a new era.

A string quartet had come to play, and the people sang "Mass of the Angels." Children sat quietly, sensing something important had happened as they watched the old in their grateful prayers.

Still in the sanctuary, Father Bruno quietly knelt before the crucifix high behind the altar. He thought of the lonely years spent looking forward to a secluded retirement: fishing on golden days in the streams of the Italian Alps, sleeping soundly on sacred nights. As I drew close, he woke from his silent reflections. "Father Bruno, people are gathering at the front of the church. They need absolution from their belief in rumors."

"You go then, Father Conley. My suspicious thoughts seemed to inevitably return when I abandoned my faith. I am not the one they want to hear from. I have failed. For good reason, I am not worthy of their trust. You go to them. They see you as a hero!"

"But, Father Bruno, you stayed with the church! In the piazza, can you hear their chant?"

He perked up to hear them calling his name through the open doors, "Father Bruno, Father Bruno!" The crowd grew louder with every minute.

"They're calling for you, father. Let them see you. Let them hear you."

He stared for a moment toward the chanting crowd and looked into my eyes; there, he seemed to take encouragement. Crossing himself, he rose to his feet and slowly moved toward the light in the piazza. He paused at the threshold to count his rosary beads and gain his composure. He appeared to the crowd in the soft light of candles. Cheers of, "Bravo," erupted from the vigil, causing humble emotions to wash over his body.

Father Bruno calmed the people with a subtle motion of his hand. They needed a prayer; they wanted a prayer from him and him alone. As he kissed his crucifix, the people instinctively knelt, and the men removed their caps. "Our Father who art in heaven, hallowed be thy name, Thy kingdom come, Thy will be done on earth as it is in heaven…and forgive us our trespasses as we forgive those who trespass against us…"

Though it had been many years for the Catholics of Florence, those who remembered its terrible past were at last ready to forgive their trespassers.

"For Thine is the kingdom and the power, and the glory, forever and ever. Amen."

The faithful waited for their priest to clarify the moment. "The Lord gave us a good priest, but we doubted him. Because of that, we wandered in the wilderness. There was a promise our sins would be forgiven. On this day, God has given us that gift. It is a reminder that He is the Giver of all. This is a time for joyous celebration! Let us restore this church in the name of *Cristo*. Let us restore the festivals, the weddings, the Christmas Mass. The doors of Sant' Ambrogio are open wide to you. Come to the church! Help us rejoice this new beginning."

High above the piazza, a chilled breeze pushed a cloud swiftly across the sky, exposing a misty half-moon. More and more, the vigil grew larger. Many came from the river district. They came wearing sweaters, and some brought blankets to wrap over their shoulders. The family of Florence huddled closely on that October night.

On the church porch, Father Bruno continued to tell the story of Father Lombardi and how he had known this good priest who had protected the church. By April, Father Bruno would finally be serenely casting for trout in the cold-water streams near Abby Monticello.

*****

Many had come to sit in the sanctuary and kneel in front of the altar. Families were slowly filling the pews that had not been filled during the disgrace. New life was breathed into the sanctuary. I felt the familiar presence, and I thought of Rosalie Campanella. I spotted her in the alcove, lighting another red votive prayer candle and wondered how many prayers she'd whispered and what comfort they had brought her in her dark years. She rose to her feet and ambled toward the open doors, where I was standing. "Who did you light the candle for, Rosalie?

"Only for Father Lombardi as so many others are lighting his candle."

I stepped back from her to see that there was a new glow, a deep happiness in her face that made her look much younger and her voice clearer and sweeter. "I am ninety-six years old. Before you were sent to my church, my thoughts were only in a dream. The young girl in me could only dream that my church would again be glorified.

"I saw you had come to recover the church, and you have. I can go to heaven knowing my grandchildren's grandchildren may be baptized in this sanctuary. There is no way to thank you for that. Father John, if you were my grandson, I would call you Christopher, the saint of travelers. You have taken the Pilgrim' Road. I see now you will follow it for many years, and that will be your life."

She continued, "But you come to my house. My family will be with me tomorrow. We will eat ravioli, the way we make it in Florenzi. I feel young again. I feel like cooking. You come to my house and give the blessing."

"I will, *Nonna*."

"Now, I must speak to the people who sing in the piazza." She appeared on the porch, where the scent of candles and flowers permeated the air.

Peering into the vigil, I saw Frances surrounded by children and glowing candles. By now, the *Santa Maria* had been prominently placed on a bronze dais.

As Rosalie Campanella began to speak, a calm came over the congregation. "I have dedicated myself to the church and the people of this church even through the years when it was almost empty. You have seen me walking there each day. I learned not to expect anyone to enter those doors while they were darkened by a cloud of disgrace. But now that the moment of truth has appeared within the sanctuary, you have come to pay reverence. I hope many have come to volunteer. The heartbeat of our church is our volunteers. We are needed to do the things that must be done to show our devotion. My heart has longed to see the Festa di Santa Maria live before I die."

Cheers erupted from the people. A high wind pushed the clouds away from a misty moon. I carefully navigated my way through the vigil toward Frances and the children who sat around her. Through a melancholy smile, she said, "Hello, Father Conley."

I could tell she knew I had truly found my calling, that whatever the future would bring, I was now wedded to my mission as a priest as she was to hers as a physician. "Frances—"

We each knew what the other was feeling. She hushed my thought. "Please, John, nothing more has to be said. In a few days, I'll be leaving the monastery, going back home to Santa Barbara for a while. Then I'll continue to find those in need of medical care. John, will you find me?"

We were not conspiring against the church when I whispered to her, "Yes, Frances, it is our secret. As the moon is now promising, I will find you."

Under the stars, songs were heard over Florence.

Reflections of Faith

So these are my final words about a journey of faith, not necessarily of my own but of those who kept it and they who gained it. For some lose faith from time to time, and it may never return. This is why I was compelled to write the story of the little church of Sant' Ambrogio. The people had come back to the church, filled its aisles on Sunday mornings, joyfully celebrated the Christmas Mass, and most of all, revel in the Festa di Santa Maria. It may have been an act of heavenly intervention or the determination and luck of a young priest. I only know God had a silent hand in it.

Soon after the rediscovery of the Granacci masterpiece, I was called by Monsignor DeLuca for another assignment. As the years have swiftly gone by, I have become my mentor's legacy. The renowned Dr. Frances George volunteers for an organization of international doctors who do what they can for forgotten people in war-torn countries. Under a shadow of grace, she has been my confidant, and I daresay, more. She has been as much an unconventional physician as I've been an unconventional priest. I have often joined her at her station as she has joined me on mine.

I write this final draft in a dusty, inadequate hospital on the Serbian border. As I pray at early dawn, an iridescent blue star appears in the eastern sky. It heightens my spirit and carries me through another sacred day.

Finito.

About the Author

Mike grew up on the family orchard near Salinas, California. He thought he'd be a farmer, never a writer, but he always wrote. In sixth grade, he wrote an article about playing music. In junior high, he wrote science fiction stories. His English teacher would read them to the class and ask if she could keep them. In high school, he dabbled in poetry and played in a popular local rock band. Things changed when his parents unexpectedly announced they were selling the ranch.

With a yearning to see other places, Mike hitchhiked from California to New Jersey and back. He enrolled at the University of Oregon in Eugene and volunteered at Whitebird Free Clinic, where he saved the life of a Hell's Angel who had overdosed on downers. He reached out to communes in the Willamette Valley as they worked on the land.

He fished salmon off Coos Bay, worked in a sawmill, been a ship clerk at the Port of Sacramento, and a real estate broker in Oklahoma. He has known travelers, fishermen, college professors, hippies, priests, holy men and rode with truckers. He has written several short stories about these experiences.

Mike visited the Vatican and Florence, Italy, where the little church of Saint Ambrogio stands. It inspired him to write this novel.

He writes because he loves telling stories about the places and people he's known. You might see them in his fictions. He writes because he loves writing and always has.

CPSIA information can be obtained
at www.ICGtesting.com
Printed in the USA
JSHW041221161222
35000JS00002B/109